To Steve & Jennifer Axelsen,
this tale told by an idiot, full of sound
and fury, signifying nothing—MC

For Matt—GR

Willy Waggledagger
BY THE PICKING OF MY NOSE

Martin Chatterton
Illustrated by Gregory Rogers

LITTLE HARE
www.littleharebooks.com

Little Hare Books
8/21 Mary Street, Surry Hills
NSW 2010 AUSTRALIA

www.littleharebooks.com

First published in 2009

National Library of Australia
Cataloguing-in-Publication entry

Chatterton, Martin.

Willy Waggledagger - by the picking of my nose / Martin
Chatterton ; illustrator, Gregory Rogers.

978 1 921272 83 7 (pbk.)

Chatterton, Martin. Willy Waggledagger ; 1.

For primary school age.

Rogers, Gregory, 1957-

823.92

Cover design by Vida Kelly
Set in 12.5/21 Stone Informal by Clinton Ellicott
Printed in Australia by Griffin Press, Adelaide

5 4 3 2 1

Contents

the sound and the furry

Anyone who has ever worn a false beard, especially a big, furry, ginger one, will know there's one thing about them that is rather annoying.

They tickle.

A lot.

Deep in the middle of the audience, eleven-year-old William Shakespeare's false beard was tickling like crazy.

Willy was wearing it because he was in disguise. And he was in disguise because Sir Victor Vile had ordered that only grown-ups were allowed inside Stratford Theatre for that night's big show. Which might not have been a problem for Willy ... except that the head-line act was the Black Skulls, the most exciting travelling theatre group in all of England.

Sir Victor or no Sir Victor, there was *no* chance of Willy letting his favourite performers play his home town without at least trying to see them. There was the music, for a start, as well as the first performance of a hot new play. If that meant strapping on a silly beard and running the risk of being nabbed by Sir Vic—not to mention Willy's equally terrifying father—then that was how it had to be. The Black Skulls would be worth the effort, Willy was sure of that.

It hadn't been easy sneaking out of home.

Willy's father, John Shakespeare, a large, red-faced man with hands the size of paddles, worked in the tannery at the side of the house. If the tannery had been confined to its own building Willy wouldn't have minded, but the garden, and much of the lower part of the house, was slowly being invaded by drying racks and boiling vats of animal skins. Willy was so used to the stink that he hardly noticed it.

But that day, with the weather being warm, the smell from the barrels was enough to make Willy gag as he tiptoed along the garden path, his disguise bundled under his tunic. He had almost made it to the gate when his father's voice boomed out of the tannery.

'Stop right there, Master Shakespeare!'

Willy dropped the disguise behind a mulberry tree a split second before his father emerged from the tannery door, a half-skinned otter dangling from his massive hand.

'Where do you think you're going? Not planning on sneaking off to the *theatre*, are you?'

Willy's father spat out the word 'theatre' like a rotten cherry. He hated the theatre almost as much as he hated parting with money, or smiling. If something didn't involve ripping the innards out of dead animals and tanning their hides, Willy's father wasn't interested. He particularly wasn't interested in airy-fairy nonsense like the *theatre*.

Willy was a disappointment to his father. He was a small, thin, dark-haired, ordinary-looking boy with a serious expression and worried eyes. Mr Shakespeare would have preferred a more *manly* son. Someone who could follow him into a proper trade.

Like tanning.

'No, sir,' said Willy leaning against the garden gate as innocently as possible. 'I'm, um, just going to ...'

'Go and skin that basket of puppies I left in the kitchen, you gleeking little gut-griping giblet,' Willy's father barked. 'Or you'll feel the back of my hand again!'

Willy looked down at his scuffed toecaps. 'Yes, sir,' he said.

He shuffled two steps towards the house, his shoulders drooping. Mr Shakespeare gave a snort of disgust, and he and the otter went back into the tannery.

The moment his father was out of sight, Willy scooped up his disguise, scrambled over the garden gate and sprinted down Stratford High Street like a greyhound out of the slips. He'd been spanked so often that one more spanking wouldn't make much difference. Not even his father on the warpath was going to keep Willy out of the theatre that day.

And now here he was, right in the middle of the action. Not long to wait.

Willy reached under his beard, scratched his chin for the twentieth time and wobbled on the stilts he'd made to give him some height. He steadied himself against the back of the man in front. The stilts—two thick blocks of wood strapped to his feet and hidden by his father's best long black cloak—made it hard to walk. Willy was glad the theatre was full. The closely packed crowd made it easier to stay upright.

Willy squinted at the posh part of the theatre, where, in the gilded Royal Box almost overhanging the stage, Her Majesty Queen Elizabeth was sitting, her face a solid mask of white make-up. Standing next to her was Sir Victor Vile, the richest man in Stratford, owner of the fiercest whiskers in all of the realm, and Commander of Her Majesty's Codpieces, the much-feared Royal Protection Squad. He glared down at the audience, looking as though he was sucking on a lemon.

A trumpet blast brought Willy's attention back to the stage.

'Your Majesty, Lords, Ladies and Gentle-men, please welcome onstage England's finest ventriloquist, Minty "The Mouth" Macvelli!'

A thin, rather nervous-looking man dressed in black appeared from behind a curtain carrying a wooden doll dressed exactly like him.

The audience didn't applaud.

'Good evening,' he said. He bowed, sat on a stool and put the doll on his knee. 'I'm here tonight with my little friend, Minimac, to get you in the mood for the Black Skulls. Isn't that right, Minimac?'

'Suppose so,' said the doll.

Even with his view partly blocked by a man in a wide-brimmed hat, Willy could see that Minty Macvelli's lips moved whenever the doll spoke. He was a lousy ventriloquist.

And his jokes weren't much good, either.

'I saw a funny thing on the way in to the theatre tonight,' said Minty. 'Two cannibals were eating a clown. One said to the other: "Does this taste funny to you?"'

'Oh, my aching sides,' said Minimac.

'Did you hear about the invisible man who married the invisible woman?' said Minty.

7

'Yes,' said Minimac. 'Their kids were nothing much to look at.'

A smelly cabbage flew past Willy's left ear and hit Minty Macvelli on the head.

'Rubbish!' shouted a voice. 'Gerroff, you scutter!'

'Who threw that?' snapped the doll, its wooden face swivelling as it surveyed the audience. 'How dare y——'

Willy wasn't the only one who thought the opening act needed more work. A hail of rotten fruit, old fish heads and various other stinky objects rained down on the stage. Minty Macvelli removed part of a turnip from his ear and scuttled off stage with as much dignity as he could muster.

Which wasn't much.

The flaming torches in the theatre were put out and there was a roar from the audience. Willy found himself being pushed towards the stage as the crowd behind him surged forward.

A tingle ran down his spine. Or possibly a rat: it was hard to tell, so closely packed was the crowd. Whatever it was, Willy knew one thing: he wouldn't have swapped places with *anyone*.

He was so close to the action he could feel the heat from the footlights. A huge, scruffy Black Skulls technician scrabbled across the front of the stage and, with a few well-placed shades, plunged the theatre into complete darkness. The audience whooped and clapped.

This was it!

'Go Black Skulls!' yelled a voice from the back. *'All right!'*

'Whoo-hoo!' A bearded man in a battered leather jerkin raised his fist. The blonde woman sitting on his shoulders shook her arms and threw her wimple at the stage.

There was a moment of silence.

Then a single white spotlight cut through the dark and lit up a figure standing centre stage, fiddle in one hand, bow in the other. It was Elbows McNamara, the Irish wonder-kid of fiddling. He drew back his arm and began to play, his nimble fingers dancing across the strings, faster, faster, and then faster still until, just as Willy thought his ears might melt, a cymbal crashed and the stage exploded in an eye-popping flash of blinding white light. In the centre of the explosion, a man catapulted upwards from below the stage and landed catlike on the boards.

The crowd went crazy.

Dressed from head to toe in black, Olivier 'Olly' Thesp, lead performer with the Black Skulls, swaggered towards the front of the stage and placed one long leather boot on the prompt box, the light dancing across the silver rings in his ears and nose. Willy could clearly see Olly's famous skull-ring gleaming on his right hand as he leaned forward, glaring at the audience as if daring them not to applaud.

Willy roared.

The crowd roared.

Olly swung his custom-made black lute into a playing position, raised a jewelled hand high, then windmilled it down across the strings. A crashing chord bounced out through the theatre and he took off.

As he whirled across the stage, Olly's braided hair flew behind him while he thrashed the lute to within an inch of its life. As he caroomed past Willy, his boot brushed against Willy's outstretched hand.

I'm never going to wash that hand again, thought Willy. Then he remembered that he never washed it anyway.

Olly returned to the front of the stage and stood, legs apart, in front of the voice-amplifier cone that was perched at head height on a stand.

'*They say I was born a travelling man!*' he bellowed. '*I do all the travelling one man can!*'

Willy whooped. 'Travelling Man' was one of

his favourites. His father had clonked him on the back of the head more than once for whistling it at the dinner table. Willy wished *he* was a travelling man. That way he could put as much distance between himself and his father as he possibly could. Then he shoved the thought to the back of his mind. He didn't want to waste time thinking about his father.

The crowd had become a solid mass of bouncing, dancing people. Even the Queen was tapping a diamond-encrusted claw on the arm of her seat, and cracking her make-up with what might have been a smile.

The Black Skulls pounded through the rest of their opening set, playing all of Willy's favourites: 'The Ten Pests', 'Rome, Oh and Julie's Hat', 'Do Nothing About Much', 'The Version of Menace'. It was fantastic. It was wonderful. And, all too soon, the musical section was over. The Black Skulls dropped their instruments and left the stage, the cheers of the crowd shaking the old timbers of the theatre.

After a few minutes of clapping and stamping, the applause was replaced by an excited buzz of chatter.

'Weren't they great?'

'Awesome, man, completely awesome!'

'He looked at me, he did!'

'Anyone need a flagon of mead?'

Willy sighed deeply and wiped his brow. It had been even better than he'd imagined. He bought himself a bag of larks' tongues and waited for the play to begin. According to the town crier he'd heard yesterday, it promised to be a rip-roaring ghost story called *The Sheeted Dead*.

Twenty-five minutes later, Willy, along with the rest of the crowd, watched spellbound as Olly Thesp, completely transformed from the braided whirlwind who had been pounding out the songs earlier, played to perfection the role of a terrified prince.

Everyone's eyes were locked on him.

Except for Sir Victor's.

Sir Victor, who, like Willy's father, was not a big fan of the theatre—or any kind of fun—was instead scanning the audience for that most disgusting of creatures: boys.

Sir Victor loathed boys.

Nasty, unwashed, little urchins they were, always poking their horrid little noses and eeny-meeny little fingers into things. As his eyes roamed across the audience, Sir Victor suddenly stiffened, like a terrier who had caught the scent of a rat.

His moustache quivered. If his instincts were right, there was something strange in the audience. Something that didn't look natural. Something orange.

It was Willy's beard.

In all the excitement, Willy's fake beard

had twisted around and was now perched on top of his head.

Sir Victor turned to the two Codpieces who stood guard behind the Queen.

'There, underneath that ginger thing,' he hissed through clenched teeth. 'A disgusting boy has wormed its way into my performance! Bring it to me at once!'

Willy, unaware of the position of his beard, was completely caught up in the play when, without warning, a meaty hand clamped onto his shoulder. Willy knew it was bad news— a meaty hand on the shoulder always was. He spun around and found himself staring into the face of one of Sir Victor's very ugliest Codpieces.

''Avin' fun are we, sir?' the ugly face said. 'Isn't it a bit late for you?'

'No!' squeaked Willy. 'I mean, no!' he added, dropping his voice down to somewhere around his knees. 'I don't know what you mean. I'm a grown-up. A *man*. I like, er, *beer* . . . and, um, stuff like that. And I can stay up as late as I like!' Willy pointed at his chin. 'I have a beard!'

The Codpieces sniggered and stared at Willy's false beard wobbling on top of his head. 'Yeah, you do,' said one of them. 'But it seems to 'ave decided it'd rather be an 'at. Now come along wiv us, you little whelp.'

'Look over there!' shouted Willy, pointing. 'The Queen's knickers are on fire!'

The two ugly Codpieces fell for the oldest trick in the book—Codpieces not being noted for their brain power—and Willy got off his stilts, dropped to all fours into the unspeakable filth on the floor of the theatre and crawled as fast as he could through the forest of legs.

Meanwhile, a ghostly white figure drifted down from the darkness above the stage.

'Oh, what dread-bolted creature is this I see before me?' whispered Olly Thesp. He held out

his hands towards the ghost. The audience was enthralled but Willy couldn't waste time listening. He scrambled to the back of the theatre and stood up.

It was a bad move.

'There 'e is!' bellowed a Codpiece, his voice booming across the silent theatre. 'Quick, cut the little runt off!'

Onstage, Olly stumbled over his line. He peered out into the crowd, his eyes narrowed.

'Shush!' hissed a large number of people. 'Keep quiet!'

The Codpieces ploughed straight through the audience like bulls through a field of wheat. Willy hoped they were too far away to catch him. He lunged towards the theatre door.

And ran smack into a large, smelly and familiar stomach.

With a sinking feeling, Willy knew without looking that he'd run into his father.

'So this is what you get up to when you're supposed to be at home, William Shakespeare?' his father bawled. 'You think those puppies will skin themselves, eh?'

'Shush!' said the audience. A carrot bounced off Mr Shakespeare's head.

Willy could swear there was steam coming out of his father's ears. He gulped. 'I . . .'

But Mr Shakespeare was already unbuckling his thick leather belt, the one he used for extra-special spankings.

Willy didn't wait to find out what would happen next. With a bloodthirsty father in front, and a troupe of ugly Codpieces coming up fast from behind, there was only place left to go.

Up.

Stratford Theatre was on two levels. Most of the audience stood on the ground level looking up at the stage. Above that level was a balcony with rows of benches to sit on. The very poshest seats, and the boxes that the real toffs used, jutted out over either side of the stage. Great big red velvet curtains, held back by fat golden ropes, hung down from the balcony to hide the support pillars. While his father fumbled with his belt, Willy leapt up and grabbed hold of one of these ropes, shinning upwards just as a Codpiece lunged for his ankles.

'Gotcha!' snarled the Codpiece as his fingers closed around Willy's leg.

With a desperate kick, Willy knocked the man's fingers away and dragged himself up the rope. He made it to the balcony and dropped gratefully over the side into the lap of Mrs Emily Butterworth, the wife of Stratford's leading undertaker. She squealed loudly.

'Sorry,' said Willy, untangling himself from Mrs Butterworth's skirts.

Mr Butterworth, a hugely fat man, heaved himself upright and threw himself at Willy.

Willy rolled backwards and half-hopped, half-stumbled his way to the side of the balcony.

'Grab him!' yelled people in the audience.

Willy headed for the nearest door and found himself in the corridor that ran along the back of the box seats. At one end was a stairway. Willy heard his father and the Codpieces racing up the stairs towards him. He ran to the other end of the corridor, quietly opened the last door, slipped inside and closed it behind him.

Bad choice.

He was in the Queen's box.

Fortunately for Willy, the two Codpieces who would normally be guarding the Queen were now busy chasing after him. Equally fortunately, neither the Queen nor Sir Victor had heard Willy come into the box. They were standing at the front of the box looking down at Olly Thesp, who was trying his best to get the play back on track. But that was as far as the good news went. With only seconds before he was discovered, Willy needed somewhere to hide, and quick. His eyes darted around the tiny box.

Nothing.

And then he saw it.

His last chance. It was a big risk—a very big risk—but, with the enemy closing in, Willy didn't have much choice. He quietly slid into the only hiding place available and held his breath.

There was a soft tap at the door. 'Beggin' yer pardon, Yer Majesty, Sir Victor,' said a Codpiece.

Willy's father tried to push through but was held back by the other Codpiece.

'What is it, you misbegotten mumble-mews?' snapped Sir Victor.

The Codpiece looked around the box, a puzzled expression on his knobbly face. 'Well, Sir, Ma'am, it's jist that a boy woz seen henterin' the Royal Box, like.'

'My boy!' spluttered Willy's father. 'And he is in for the spanking of his life!'

Sir Victor scowled. 'In *here*? Are you mad, man? Where could anyone possibly hide in this place?'

Sir Victor had a point. There was, quite simply, nowhere for anyone to hide, not even a small boy.

The Queen, not happy at having her entertainment interrupted, did not look amused.

'The Queen is not amused, Vile,' she said in the voice that she usually used for sending people to have their heads removed. 'One is *enjoying* oneself and one would like to *continue* enjoying oneself without interruption!'

'My humblest apologies, Your Majesty,' Sir Victor managed to croak. 'You may rest assured that the ... erm, boy responsible for this will be ...'

From his hiding place almost directly underneath the Queen's bum, where he was concealed by her large skirts, Willy listened as Sir Victor described in painful detail what was waiting for him once he was found.

'There's something fishy going on here, Your Majesty,' Sir Victor went on. 'I can *smell* a child in here. Those nasty little things are worse than *vermin*!'

The Queen, a very clean woman who bathed once a year whether she needed to or not, raised her eyebrows in horror.

At that moment a stray whisker from Willy's beard—still on top of his head—found its way through a small rip in the royal knickers and brushed against the royal bum. The Queen leapt up, screaming at the top of her lungs, and toppled backwards. Sir Victor, moving like moustachioed lightning, flung himself underneath the Queen to cushion her fall. She landed squarely on his back.

'*Oooof!*' gasped Sir Victor.

'*Aaargh!*' screamed the Queen as Willy

emerged from her skirts, his face wrapped in part of her underskirt. 'A ghost!'

'Lumme!' said the Codpiece.

Willy disentangled himself.

'That's no ghost!' shouted Willy's father from the doorway. 'That's my good-for-nothing son!'

Sir Victor removed the Queen's knee from his ear as politely as he could and pointed at Willy. 'Don't just stand there, you buffoon! Get him!'

Once again Willy had nowhere to go.

Between him and the door: the Codpiece, Sir Victor, the Queen, his father. Behind him: the edge of the box, which hung over the audience and part of the stage—a sheer drop, and not a soft landing to be had.

'C'mere!' snarled the Codpiece, lunging at Willy.

'No, thanks,' said Willy, wriggling out of his grasp.

He sprang onto the lip of the box and jumped.

Olly was coming to the end of the ghost scene.

'Away, oh noxious beastie of the night!' Olly wailed, his arms outstretched, his eyes closed.

Above him, from out of the darkness, came Willy. The billowing cloak slowed his fall, but not by much, and Willy's toes connected with Olly's softest body parts with the impact of a hammer hitting a watermelon. Olly Thesp gave a bloodcurdling screech and fell to the floor in a crumpled heap. The crowd, thinking this was part of the show, went bananas. (Or would have done if they had known what bananas were.)

They giggled. They chuckled. They howled. Small boys cried tears of joy behind their fake beards. Old ladies dabbed at their eyes. The Mayor of Stratford had to be revived with a glass of water.

Olly Thesp staggered to his feet with Willy's beard clinging to his face. He ripped it off and threw it at Willy.

'This is an absolute outrage, sir!' Olly howled, hobbling offstage.

Willy had no time to think about what he'd done. Three more Codpieces and his fire-breathing father were clomping their way through the audience towards the stage.

'Don't you dare move, William Shakespeare!' roared Mr Shakespeare, waving his belt above his head.

Willy sprinted into the wings and ran straight into a brick wall.

'Oi!' said the brick wall, which wasn't really a brick wall. 'Watch where yer goin'! You almost knocked old Yorick down!'

It was the big scruffy man who had been fixing the stage lights earlier. Up close he was like a shaggy ox, all hair, leather and a strange, not altogether unpleasant, smell. Yorick noisily blew his nose on a large black handkerchief.

'Looks like yer in a speck of trouble,' said Yorick, peering past Willy's shoulder at Sir Victor, the Codpieces and Willy's father. 'Now, let's see wot we can do about that. Wot's yer name, by the way?'

'William,' said Willy. 'William Shakespeare. But everyone calls me . . .'

'Never mind all that,' said Yorick, as he spotted the first Codpiece clambering onstage. He grabbed Willy by the scruff of his neck, dragged him back into the shadows between two large stage flats and stood him in front of a black screen. 'Stand 'ere and say nuffink.'

Yorick inspected his gigantic black handkerchief, gave it a quick shake, and draped it over Willy.

Against the black background, and covered by Yorick's handkerchief in the shadows, Willy was almost invisible. Which was just as well. He tried to stop breathing.

'You there, hairy stage person!' snarled Sir Victor Vile as he and the others barged backstage and skidded to a halt only inches from Willy's hiding place.

'Yes?' said Yorick.

'A revolting *boy* ran in here some seconds past,' said Sir Victor. 'Where is he? And no funny business, mind! The rough-hewn scoundrel is wanted for high treason. He's due for the chop!'

'And the spanking of his life!' added Willy's father.

Underneath the cloth, Willy shuddered.

Sir Victor shot a withering look at Mr Shakespeare and leaned closer to Yorick. 'And anyone foolish enough to help him is also due for the chop!' he hissed. 'Understand, yokel?'

Yorick pointed in the direction of the stage doors that led to a narrow alley behind the theatre. 'I fink 'e went that ways, Yer Honour.

Fast, 'e woz! Like a whippet! I reckon 'e's 'alfway up 'Igh Street by now.'

Sir Victor, the Codpieces and Willy's father clattered through the big wooden doors, out of the theatre and down the alley. Yorick watched them go, shaking his head slowly.

He bent down and tapped Willy on the head.

'Just keep yer 'ead down fer a few more minutes, Shufflespear, Shakesword, Waggle-dagger ... wotever yer name is!' he said. 'I'm orf to make sure this crowd don't rip the theatre down.'

Willy nodded underneath his nice safe black handkerchief. He was beginning to like it there, and he decided he might never come out. If he stayed invisible, maybe things wouldn't get any stranger.

2

Is this a Booger I see Before Me?

Things got stranger.

Almost as soon as Yorick left, Willy heard voices coming from somewhere behind him.

'*Double*, darling. I said, *double*!' said one voice. 'Let it bubble. Add more frog or there'll be trouble.'

'Clove of garlic, leg of fowl, eye of newt and a fillet of fenny snake,' said another. 'That's more like it! Now bring it to the boil and let it simmer.'

Willy blinked. Unless he was mistaken these people sounded just like . . . witches!

He peeped out from under the handkerchief.

Not a Codpiece in sight. And no sign of his father, or Sir Victor.

Willy dropped Yorick's handkerchief on the floor and crept towards the voices. He tiptoed down a small corridor crowded with theatrical junk until he found himself at the doorway to what must have been the theatre kitchen.

It was a dark, smoky room with a huge fireplace set into the back wall. Three women were gathered in front of a large pot hung over a crackling fire, their shadows dancing across the ceiling.

They looked exactly how Willy imagined witches would look—wrinkled, with large noses and long tangled hair—although they were a bit better dressed than he had expected. With their crisp white aprons, they looked more like cooks than witches. One of them was busy ripping the innards out of an albatross. Another was sprinkling a handful of white crystals into the pot, while the third dipped a wooden spoon into the brown mixture.

The third woman turned with the spoon in her hand and offered it to someone Willy couldn't see. 'What do you think?' she said.

Willy inched forward and saw a man sitting at a kitchen table. It was the ventriloquist who'd been driven offstage earlier, Minty Macvelli.

Minty took the spoon and put it in his mouth. 'Not bad at all, Henrietta,' he said. 'Do I detect grilled wolverine kidneys? A hint of marinated bear liver?'

'Close,' said Henrietta. 'I'm using a puree of mink brain. Gives it that lovely sharp tang.'

These women definitely aren't witches, Willy thought.

'Sounds disgusting,' said Minimac. 'You might as well be eating dead-dog stew!'

Minty Macvelli looked sadly at his doll. 'Now, now, Minimac, there's no need to be rude to the nice ladies.'

Minimac gave a disgusted snort. 'Spineless as always, Macvelli,' he snarled. 'No wonder Olivier Thesp walks all over you!'

Even though Willy could see Minty Macvelli's lips move as Minimac spoke, it was still hard to remember that the doll wasn't real.

'Sorry about Minimac,' said Minty to Henrietta. 'He's in a bad mood tonight.'

'That's all right, my love,' she replied. 'We get all kinds of weirdos in our line of work.' She winked at the other women. 'Right, girls?'

Henrietta turned back to the pot and filled a large bowl. 'There you go,' she said, plonking it in front of Minty. 'Get that inside you. It'll put hair on your chest.'

As Minty dug into the stew, Willy realised how hungry he was. He had forgotten his lunch in his hurry to get out of the house so, apart from that tiny bag of larks' tongues, he hadn't eaten since breakfast. His stomach growled loudly.

'Did you hear that?' said Minty, glancing in Willy's direction.

Willy turned to run and crashed into a stack of stage weapons. They fell noisily and he tumbled into the kitchen in an avalanche of fake swords, axes and spears.

Minty squealed and dived under the table.

Henrietta bent down and hoisted Willy to his feet.

'Hello,' she said. 'The name's Henrietta. Henrietta Hag. These are my sisters, Hermione and Hortense.'

'Willy,' said Willy, picking bits of bread from his tunic. 'Willy ... erm ... Waggle-dagger. Pleased to meet you, Mistress Hag.'

'Call me Henrietta, please,' she said as she peered under the table at Minty. 'Nothing to be scared of, dearie. It's just a boy.'

Minty crawled out. He brushed the dust from his knees with one hand and set Minimac straight on the other.

'One can't be too careful these days,' he said. 'Boys can be dangerous! Look at what that urchin did to Olly. Hey! Wait a minute! You're that kid who smacked Olly in the ...' Minty stepped forward and shook Willy's hand. 'Put it there, kid! Anyone who can wipe the smile off that fool's face is all right by me! I haven't laughed so hard since Yorick put chilli powder in Olly's underpants.'

'I didn't mean to land on him,' said Willy. 'He's my hero!'

'Yes, yes, of course he is,' said Minty. 'He's the brightest star in all of England!'

Minimac thrust his wooden face close to Minty's. 'Who are you fooling?' he said. 'If Thesp dropped dead tomorrow you'd throw a party.'

'You're joking, right?' gasped Willy.

Minty nodded. 'That's right, he's joking. *Har har!*'

'Whatever you say,' said Minimac.

'Anyway,' said Minty, sitting back at the table, 'even if something bad did happen to Olly, what difference would it make?'

'Like to find out?' said Henrietta. She whipped a business card out of her apron pocket and waved it under Minty's nose.

'*Les Trois Hags*,' Willy read over Minty's shoulder. '*High-class catering. Nose-readings. All occasions. Theatricals a speciality.*'

Henrietta sat down next to Minty. 'Do you want to find out what life's got in store for you?' she said. 'Easily done with a spot of nose-reading.'

'Nose-reading?' squeaked Minty, as if she'd suggested they get married.

Henrietta leaned close to Minty and traced a crooked finger down his nose.

'Yes, dearie,' she said in the sort of voice you might use with an elderly relative who thought he was the Emperor of China. 'I'm a fortune teller. Just like a palm reader, except my particular speciality is noses. Schnozzes, conks, beaks, whatever you want to call them.'

The closer Henrietta leaned towards Minty, the further he leaned back, until he was holding on to the edge of the table to stop his chair from toppling. 'It's not my cup of tea,' he said. 'I don't really believe in, um . . . y'know, fortune-telling and all that nons . . . stuff.'

'It's only a bit o' harmless fun!' said Henrietta. 'Don't be afeared.' She peered intently at Minty's nose.

Her sisters gathered round to watch.

'She's very good,' said Hermione, smiling at Minty.

'The best nose-reader north of Glastonbury,' added Hortense.

Willy couldn't imagine there would be much competition in the world of nose-reading, but he jostled closer. He'd never seen a nose-reading before.

'Are you after a reading, too, youngster?'

Hortense asked him. 'No charge. I'm still training.'

'No, thanks,' Willy said. He clapped a hand over his nose and shook his head vigorously.

Meanwhile, Henrietta was peering closely at Minty's nose. Suddenly, without warning, she shot out a thin finger and, before Minty could say a word, stuck it up his left nostril.

'*Nyaaaaarrrrglynyyyyynah!*' Minty yowled. 'What do you think you're doing?'

'Quiet,' whispered Henrietta. She waggled her finger back and forth, then pulled out a small green booger.

'*Eeeeuw*, that's just disgusting,' said Willy, backing away before Hortense got any ideas.

'*Yeeeuch!*' said Minimac.

Minty didn't say anything. He was too shocked.

Henrietta brought the booger up close to one eye and examined it as if it was a very beautiful diamond.

'By the picking of your nose,' she murmured, 'something wicked this way goes.'

'Wicked?' said Minty, still pale with horror. His normally ghost-white skin had gone a sickly shade of green. 'What do you mean?'

Henrietta squinted at Minty and then back at the booger. 'Just a saying. Not important,' she said. 'But what *is* important is what the booger is telling me.'

Minty stiffened in his chair. Henrietta had his full attention. 'Telling you? What do you mean, "telling you"?'

Henrietta paused dramatically. 'This booger is predicting you will become the stand-in for Olivier Thesp!'

'Stand-in? For Olly?' said Willy. 'You're joking! No one can replace Olly Thesp! He's *Olly Thesp*!'

Henrietta shook her head. 'I never joke about boogers, duckie.'

Minimac chuckled woodenly. 'So if, for

example, something nasty was to happen to Olivier—like getting booted in the unmention-ables—then old Minty here would become . . .'

'Lead performer with the Black Skulls.' said Willy.

'The boogers never lie,' said Henrietta. 'Never.'

Without warning, Hermione suddenly grabbed hold of Willy. 'What's this little feller's nose got to say?'

Willy struggled but Hermione had a grip of steel. She was clearly hell-bent on practising her nose-reading and, without hesitation, she extended a wizened finger and scraped a dried piece of booger off Willy's nose.

'Interesting,' she said. 'This booger isn't yours. It's Yorick's. What it's doing on *your* nose, I really don't know. Make a habit of picking other people's noses, do you?'

'*No!*' cried Willy, outraged.

And, he thought, it was a bit rich Hermione

teasing *him* about picking other people's noses when she did it for a living!

Willy's mind flashed back to Yorick's hand-kerchief, the one he'd been hiding under. That must have been how Yorick's booger ended up on Willy's nose. Willy almost barfed.

Minimac waggled his little wooden head. 'What about Yorick? He's not going to be the lead performer, too, is he?'

'Not performing,' murmured Hermione turning the booger this way and that. 'But it does look like he will discover the greatest theatrical talent of all time.'

There was a moment's silence.

'*Yorick?*' said Minty at last. 'Big, hairy feller, wears a lot of smelly leather? Are you *sure*?'

Henrietta nodded. 'Quite sure.'

Willy gently pulled his nose out of Henrietta's grasp and backed away. He really didn't want her to read his own boogers. Apart from anything else, they might say he was going to spend the rest of his life skinning animals in Stratford. Willy didn't think he could bear hearing that.

'And you discovered all this from a little lump of, er ... snot?' Willy said, his hand curled protectively around his nose.

Hermione went back to the fireplace, reached for a ladle and filled another bowl with stew. 'Like Henrietta said, the boogers never lie,' she said, handing the bowl to Willy.

Minty Macvelli sneaked a glance across the table at Willy. His ferrety eyes glowed. 'I think you just might be my good luck charm, Mr Waggledagger,' he said. 'In fact, I *know* you are my good luck charm.'

'But I didn't mean to biff Olly!' said Willy. 'I was just trying to escape from Sir Victor and my father!'

'Of course you were,' said Minty with a sly wink. 'And along the way you copped Olly a good one. I'm going to keep a very sharp eye on you, my friend. Look at the evidence. You turn up and, bingo, Mistress Henrietta predicts I'm going to be leading the Black Skulls!'

'But——' said Willy.

'But me no buts! You'll have to come along with us for the rest of the tour. This could be the start of a beautiful friendship.'

Willy blinked stupidly at Minty.

Had he heard right? Had Minty Macvelli just asked him to join the Black Skulls?

Willy dipped his spoon into the stew and popped a beaver liver into his mouth. He chewed thoughtfully. A life with the Skulls would mean no more Sir Victor, no more Codpieces, no more skinning animals, no more stinking tannery, no more spankings, no more father. All he had to do was steer clear of Sir Victor and his goons until the Black Skulls were out of Stratford.

It could be the answer to everything.

3

Thunder, Lightning, Rain Later

The audience had long gone and everyone connected with the Black Skulls was gathered onstage. Sir Victor and the Codpieces, along with Willy's father—according to Yorick who seemed to know everything—were still hunting for Willy in Stratford Forest. Walden Kemp, the tiny, red-faced director of the Black Skulls, paced backwards and forwards in front of Willy, his titchy boots stamping on the boards. He kept glancing at Willy and snorting like a bull, the veins on his neck pulsing dangerously.

Olivier Thesp was, as usual, centre stage. He pointed a finger at Willy, his rings rattling in fury. 'I expect that … mewling, milk-livered, measle to be removed at once!' he bellowed, his actor-voice booming around the empty theatre. *'At once!'*

He turned on his heel as smoothly as he could—his soft bits still appeared to be aching something terrible—and hobbled back to his seat, where he sat glaring at Willy.

'Be a bit difficult to boot the boy out now, Olly,' said Yorick. 'Seein' as we woz 'idin' 'im. Leastways that's 'ow it'll seem to Sir Vic. Don't look good.'

'We weren't hiding him!' said Charlie Ginnel, the Black Skulls manager, a man as fat and large as Walden Kemp was small and skinny. *'You* were!' He wiped his balding brow with a green silk handkerchief.

'Seemed the gentlemanly fing to do,' muttered Yorick. 'Besides, wot you goin' to do about it? Sack me as well?'

Charlie glared at him. 'Don't tempt me,

Yorick. This tickle-brained fool ruined tonight's performance!'

'Can I just say——' said Willy.

'No, you flaming well can't!' yelled Walden Kemp, his eyes popping. His head looked like it might explode at any moment. 'We'll be lucky if Olly recovers in time for the next show!'

Charlie looked sadly at Willy and shook his head. 'We can't afford to mess up another performance, not with the Queen around.'

'What about Minty?' blurted Willy.

'What *are* you talking about, you puny puttock?' Walden shouted.

Willy smiled nervously. Maybe he'd already said too much. 'Minty,' he said. 'I just meant that he ... I mean, perhaps he could ... maybe stand in for Mr Thesp? He looks just like him. He's even got the same sort of beard.'

Walden Kemp stopped pacing and scowled at Willy, his head on one side.

'Minty?' said Charlie, scratching one of his

chins. 'I hadn't really thought of that.' He glanced at Walden and raised an eyebrow.

'It's an outrageous idea. Ridiculous. Lunatic. Insane,' cried Walden. 'It just might work.'

'What?' shrieked Olly. 'Minty Macvelli replacing the irreplaceable Olivier Thesp?'

'Now, now, Olly,' said Charlie. 'No one's saying he's going to *replace* you. He would only be your stand-in, in case anything went, you know, wrong.'

'It won't be forever,' said Walden.

'Wot 'ave we got to lose?' said Yorick. 'Olly might not like it, but young Waggledagger 'ere 'as got a point.'

Minty, looking like a cat who'd found a sneaky way into a creamery, sprang to his feet. 'He's right! I know all the lines, all the moves! And my singing—well, let's just say it has to be heard to be believed!'

Charlie rubbed his pudgy hands together. 'I dunno . . .' he said slowly.

'I can't believe what I'm hearing!' said Olly. He stamped a black-booted foot. 'As if Minty could possibly replace *me*!'

Walden Kemp jerked a thumb in Willy's direction. 'Much as I hate to say it, the kid is onto something, Olly,' he said. 'Using Minty as backup would give us some breathing space.'

Charlie looked at Yorick, who gave a nod of his shaggy head. 'Looks like we have a new stand-in,' Charlie said.

'Over my dead body!' hissed Olly. He stalked up to Minty and prodded him in the chest with a finger. 'Don't get carried away, Macvelli. You're in because there's no one else, right? Just because we're getting you on stand-by doesn't mean you're suddenly the big cheese! I plan to be the lead performer round here for a long time, got it? Nothing's going to happen to me!'

'Perish the thought,' said Minty.

'Just so we understand one another,' said

Olly. He shot a poisonous glance at Willy. 'I'm going to put some ointment on my ... injuries.' He hobbled away in the direction of the dressing rooms.

Minty watched him go, a smirk spreading across his face. 'You won't regret this, Charlie!' he said as Olly disappeared from view.

'I hope that's true, Minty!' snapped Walden. He turned and scurried after Olly, waving a sheaf of scripts. 'Olly, baby! Wait!'

Charlie turned back to Willy. 'Now, what are we going to do about you?'

Yorick ambled over. 'I could really do wiv a gofer, Chaz,' he said. 'An' all this'll blow over as soon as we get out o' Stratford. You won't know the boy's 'ere.'

There was a long pause. Willy crossed his fingers and his toes. He hardly dared breathe.

'Very well,' said Charlie. 'You're in. Let's see how it goes.'

'Does this mean I can stay?' gasped Willy.

'I hope I don't regret it, but yes,' said Charlie. 'It's on your head, Yorick, got that?'

'Wouldn't 'ave it any other way, Charlie.' Yorick smiled and gave Willy the thumbs-up.

'I don't believe it,' said Minimac. 'This young sprout cops Olivier in the unmentionables and, *bish bosh*, Minty here gets the chance to be Thesp's stand-in?'

'That's about the size of it,' said Charlie. 'The show must go on.'

'Personally,' muttered Minimac, 'I'd pay good money to watch the boy catch Olly in the unmentionables again.'

'He's not the only one, from what I hear,' said a voice from the shadows at the back of the theatre. A man stepped forward. 'Norm Widemouth, chief entertainment reporter, *Stratford Evening News*.'

'Oh, sweet potato pie!' muttered Charlie. 'A reporter! That's all I need.'

'Just one question for our listeners, if you

don't mind, Mr Ginnell,' said Widemouth as he picked his way through the rubbish left behind by the audience. 'I'm sure they'll all want to know the truth behind tonight's rumours.'

'The truth? That'd be a first from you blokes,' growled Yorick.

The jab rolled off Norm Widemouth like water off a greased duck wearing an oilskin jacket and carrying an umbrella. 'Now, the big question is,' he said, taking out a roll of parchment and plucking a quill from behind his ear, 'what play will you be performing for Her Majesty at Vile Towers tomorrow?'

Charlie Ginnell looked puzzled. 'Vile Towers? What do you mean?'

Norm Widemouth stuck his quill back behind his ear and pulled a second roll of parchment from inside his jerkin. 'I bumped into a Codpiece bringing this into the theatre,' he said, 'and took the liberty of offering my services as messenger boy. This message is from the Queen herself.'

He unrolled the second parchment, turned it the right way round and squinted at it.

'She's requested—well, it's more of an order, to be honest—that the Black Skulls appear for her at Sir Vic's place tomorrow. Seems she enjoyed the performance and wants to see it all again. The boy catching Olly in the funda-mentals was the funniest thing she's seen in a long time. If you let me break the news, I'll make sure you get some good publicity.'

Charlie Ginnell's eyes lit up. A private gig for the Queen was not to be sniffed at. Perhaps the night hadn't been such a disaster after all. 'Publicity, eh? Get your quill ready, Norm, you've got an exclusive!'

Norm Widemouth retrieved his quill, licked the end and started writing.

*

Twenty minutes later, Willy was standing in the doorway of the Stratford Theatre alongside Minty and Yorick, watching Norm Widemouth's late evening bulletin and trying to keep out of the rain.

'HEAR YE! HEAR YE! QUEEN'S BUM TICKLED BY MYSTERY BEARD AT THEATRE! BLACK SKULLS IN ROYAL COMMAND PERFORMANCE SHOCK! FULL STORY TO FOLLOW! NOW TO THE WEATHER! EARLY MIST WILL BE FOLLOWED BY PERIODS OF ...'

Despite the drizzle, a crowd had gathered as Norm bawled the headline stories from on top of an upturned bucket in the middle of High Street.

'You see that?' said Minty, his eyes gleaming. 'That's pure box-office gold, that is, Waggledagger!'

He pointed to the ticket cart where Charlie Ginnell was doing a brisk trade in Black Skull merchandise. Olivier Thesp beards were going

like hot cakes. And Olivier Thesp cakes were going like hot beards.

Charlie caught sight of Willy and winked. Ever since the Queen's request for another show, Charlie seemed to have completely forgotten he had ever considered kicking Willy out.

'First rule of theatre, Waggledagger,' said Yorick. 'It's all about bums on seats.'

Willy was too excited to reply. The last few hours had been the most thrilling of his life. He'd been to a Black Skulls performance, hidden under the Queen's skirts, had a booger-reading and—according to Minty—was responsible for Minty's promotion to Olly's stand-in.

If I play my cards right, thought Willy, and if Minty and Yorick help me to hide out for long enough, I might be able to say goodbye to Stratford and my father's tannery for ever.

There was only one fly in the ointment.

Willy was dressed as a girl.

'I feel ridiculous,' he muttered, and waggled a yellow pigtail. 'I mean, look at it. I don't even *look* like a girl!'

'True,' said Minty. 'You look like a bit of a nightmare, to be honest, Waggledagger. But nightmare or not, the dress stays. I don't want my lucky charm getting pinched by the Codpieces.'

'Sounds painful,' said Yorick. 'But Minty's right about them Codpieces.' He cocked a massive thumb down High Street. 'Check this lot out.'

Three Codpieces were splashing through the puddles up High Street towards the theatre. Willy shuddered and drew a woolly pigtail across his face. The Codpieces scanned the crowd suspiciously.

'Easy, young feller,' murmured Yorick. He tipped a hand to his cap as the Codpieces drew level. 'Evenin' gents,' he said. 'Out fer a stroll in this fine weather?'

'Very funny,' said the biggest Codpiece. Rain dripped from his large nose as he frowned at Willy. Willy twirled his pigtail and simpered. The Codpiece grunted and, with a last hard look at Yorick, lurched on up the street.

'That disguise doesn't seem like such a bad idea now, does it?' said Minty. 'All you have to do is lay low for a bit, learn something about the business, and before you know it you'll be a member of the finest performing troupe in all of England. What do you think, Yorick?'

Yorick idly untangled a piece of string from his beard. 'I fink we should get back inside. Willy's get-up might fool a Codpiece but we shouldn't take too many chances. Not until the dust's settled, anyways. Besides, this rain's gettin' on me nerves.'

'You're right, Yorick,' said Minty. 'Anyone fancy a bite to eat? I think there's some of that stew left in the kitchen.'

They left Norm Widemouth shouting out the archery results, slipped back inside and headed for the kitchen. The three hags were dozing under the table. Willy was slightly surprised they hadn't flown up to the rafters for their nap. Yorick wasted no time in ladling out a giant bowlful of stew and starting in on it.

'Oi!' said a voice from inside a large box on the table.

Minty opened the box and picked up Minimac.

'Don't mind me,' said the doll, as Minty put him on his lap. 'I'll just lie there while you hang out with your brand-new friend.' He swivelled his wooden head towards Willy. 'The hero of the hour!' he said. 'Don't you look sweet?'

'Easy, Minimac,' said Minty. 'It's thanks to Master Waggledagger that I'm Olly's stand-in! Just like the ladies predicted, eh?'

Minimac nodded slyly. 'But that's not all they said, was it?'

'Wot's 'e talkin' about?' said Yorick, his shaggy head lifting from the bowl and his spoon pausing mid-scoop.

Minty showed a sudden interest in the state of Minimac's hair. 'Nothing,' he said.

Minimac snorted. 'They predicted,' he said, 'that as well as Minty becoming Olly's stand-in, he'd also become lead performer one day. Isn't that right, Macvelli?'

Minty shrugged, rolled his eyes and inspected his fingernails. 'S'pose,' he said. ''Course it doesn't *mean* anything. Not yet.'

'So,' said Minimac, 'if, God forbid, anything *unfortunate* was to happen to Olly, then old Minty here—along with yours truly—would be in line for the top job! The headline act. The big cheese!'

'But nuffink's gonna happen to Olly,' growled Yorick. He picked a fat weevil from a piece of bread and bit it in two. 'Is it, Minty?'

'No, no, no, of course not!' stammered Minty. 'Olly's as fit as a flea. Go on for years most likely! People like him always do.'

'That's right,' said Yorick. 'Let's see that 'e does, eh?' He grabbed a couple of chickens and a flagon of ale from the table. 'Come on, Waggledagger. Let's take a bite o' supper and I'll show you where you can kip.'

Yorick turned and stomped towards the door, Willy trotting at his heels.

'You can say what you like, Minty,' whined Minimac, 'those hags got it right with the first prediction. Who's to say what might happen next, eh?'

Willy loosened the bodice of his gown, scratched an itch under his wig and stepped out of the kitchen.

It had been a hell of a day.

4

Careless Trifle (and Pickled Haggis)

The next day was an absolute pip. The rain clouds of the previous evening had rolled back and the sun shone down on a glorious English summer morning. Cows mooed, dewdrops glittered on the grass, bluebirds twittered on the bough. Vile Towers lay snoozing peacefully as the Black Skulls unpacked after their short trip from Stratford.

All was well with the world.

Well, almost all.

'Blasted actors!' Sir Victor Vile—his face a unhealthy dark plum colour and his temper not improved by the thought of a dull meeting he was due to attend with the Queen—barged into the Great Hall and kicked aside a pile of stage props. Willy, walking past the doorway, hitched up his skirt and jumped out of the way as a papier-mâché dragon-head skittered across the wooden floor towards him. He almost dropped the mirror Yorick had asked him to fetch.

'Can't you useless band of fops keep your piffling toys out from under my feet?' bellowed Sir Victor. 'It's bad enough I have to open up the Towers to *actors*, without tripping over all this frippery!'

Charlie and Walden, who were huddled over a script in a corner, tried to pretend they weren't there. Minty, who, for some reason, was carrying a crowbar to the back of the hall, lifted it to his eye and inspected it closely. Only Yorick—who was putting the finishing touches to a temporary stage made up of wooden boards over a complicated arrangement of trestles and beams—didn't seem to be impressed by the new arrival. He fixed the last part of the cloth that hid the skeleton of the stage from view and looked up.

Sir Victor took a step forward and skidded on a stray ginger-coloured beard that had dropped out of an opened make-up trunk. He fell flat on his behind. Willy stifled a laugh: the last thing he needed was for Sir Victor to notice him.

Sir Victor scrambled to his feet and kicked the beard as hard as he could. He opened his mouth to shout at someone—anyone would do—scowled at the beard, and then suddenly seemed to remember something.

It didn't take long for Sir Victor to put two and two together. That slimy little boy in the theatre had been wearing a beard. A ginger one! Full, Sir Victor had no doubt, of revolting child-type disease. He peered suspiciously at the assembled company.

His gaze stopped on what appeared to be a maid holding a mirror. There was, decided Sir Victor, something fishy about her.

'You there!' said Sir Victor, pointing at Willy. 'Come closer.'

Willy's stomach twisted itself into knots and he felt a strong urge to rush immediately to the nearest privy.

'Y-y-es, Your Magnificence,' he quavered, doing his best to stay calm. A hard thing to do when he was worried his bottom might explode at any minute.

Sir Victor, his fingers tapping an impatient tattoo on the handle of his sword, watched through narrowed eyes as Willy timidly approached.

'You look ... *familiar*,' he murmured. 'And quite plain, too, for a maid.' He stroked his moustache thoughtfully. 'Can't quite put my finger on it ...'

Sir Victor leaned closer to Willy.

This is it, Willy thought, nervously fingering his neck. He really hoped Sir Victor wouldn't chop his head off. He was quite attached to it.

'I've been searching for a child who looks a lot like you,' said Sir Victor. 'Except he is a boy. Searching very hard indeed. He was a disrespectful oik who upset Her Majesty and made me look like a blethering fool!'

That wouldn't be too difficult, thought Willy, but wisely kept this to himself.

'And I do not like being made to look foolish,' continued Sir Victor. 'Not One Little Bit.'

'Of course not, Your Lordship,' said Willy. 'But as you can see I'm a girl. Not a boy. A girl.'

'Ye-es, quite,' said Sir Victor. 'But there is something . . .'

Suddenly there was an almighty crash from the other side of the hall. Sir Victor whirled round, his sword halfway out of its scabbard.

Yorick stood beside the remains of a suit of armour that now lay scattered in pieces, the helmet spinning madly. 'Oops,' he said. 'Just tryin' to move this out of the way, like. Sorry, Guv.'

'You grisly grease-gripped golem!' Sir Victor roared. 'That was the suit of armour Great-Great-Uncle Montgomery wore at the Battle of Snodgrass! Put it back together exactly as you found it, or your head will be on a spike!'

There was a cough from behind Sir Victor.

Sir Victor spun around again, his sword even further out of its scabbard. A small man, with the bushiest whiskers Willy had ever seen, stood fidgeting at the doorway. It was McDivot, Sir Victor's head gardener.

'Yes, McDivot?' Sir Victor growled.

'Well, Sir,' said McDivot, in a broad Scottish accent, 'it's Ermintrude, Yir Lordship.'

'What about her?' Sir Victor snapped.

'She isnae looking herself, Sir.'

'*What?*' Sir Victor's face turned an even darker shade of purple. 'Mark my words,

McDivot, if anything happens to Ermintrude, the person responsible will feel the edge of my sword!'

'Aye, Sir,' said McDivot, nervously tugging on his whiskers.

'As soon as my meeting with Her Majesty is over,' Sir Victor carried on, 'we'll pay Ermintrude a visit and see what sort of shape you've left her in, you haggis-guzzling nincompoop! Is that clear?'

'Aye, Yir Lordship,' whispered McDivot.

Sir Victor flicked his cape over his shoulder and, with a blistering glare at Yorick, strode out of the Great Hall, McDivot following closely. As the door slammed shut behind them, everyone sprang back into action. Everyone except Minty, who stared thoughtfully at the door. Then he narrowed his eyes, slapped the crowbar he was carrying against his other hand and skulked backstage.

Willy mopped his brow with his pigtails

and let out a long sigh of relief. 'That was lucky,' he said, trotting across the hall to Yorick. 'I thought I was a goner, for sure! Just as well this suit of armour fell over.'

'Luck didn't come into it, Waggledagger,' said Yorick. 'Old Uncle Monty didn't fall. I pushed him. Misdirection, Waggledagger. The oldest theatrical trick in the book. Now, pass me that leg.'

Willy grabbed a section of armour and passed it to Yorick.

'I fort it was time fer Sir Victor to 'ave his attention elsewhere, see?' Yorick explained as he began the tricky task of reassembling Great Uncle Monty. 'Quick push on the suit of armour and *bish bosh*, Sir Victor forgets all about you. Stagecraft. It's wot makes all them preenin', puffed-up performers look good. It's wot puts the *show* into show business. Battle scene, you say? Get me six jars of tomatoes and a few 'alf coconuts and I'll make you believe you've just seen the fall of Rome!'

Willy wasn't listening. The realisation of just how dangerous it was for him to be in Vile Towers was hitting home. He absentmindedly fitted Uncle Monty's arm to Uncle Monty's knee.

Yorick pushed Willy aside and switched the arm to its proper position. 'You need to concentrate, Waggledagger.'

'Easy for you to say, Yorick,' said Willy. 'You don't have a maniac like Sir Victor after your neck.' He hitched up his skirt. '*And* you don't have to dress up like this.'

'Saved you from Sir Victor just now, didn't it?' said Yorick. He twisted Uncle Monty's helmet into place and stepped back, looking pleased with himself. 'There, good as new!'

Willy picked up the mirror he'd placed against the wall and headed for the backstage area. It took up most of the rear of the hall, and included several 'rooms' formed by a motley collection of old curtains, rugs, bits of clothing and lengths of string. Olly, of course, had a dressing room all to himself. As Willy propped the mirror beside the others he'd brought from the wagon earlier, he saw Minty lean his crowbar against a wall and slip out of the rear entrance.

Willy scooted towards the hall, almost skidding on a patch of what looked like kitchen slops that someone had spilt. He wiped the floor with a rag and trotted back to Yorick.

'What's next, boss?' said Willy.

'Snow,' said Yorick. 'Snow is wot's next. Look lively, we got to make sure the snow machine's workin' proper.' He sniffed the air. 'Can you smell summink, Waggledagger?'

Willy held up the rag. 'Spot of cleaning,' he said. 'Now, where's this snow?'

The snow was needed for a scene in the play that was set on a lonely heath where Olly had to battle through a blizzard. Creating the blizzard, Yorick explained, was Willy's job.

Willy followed Yorick to a complicated bit of equipment hidden behind a painted rock at the side of the stage. It was a big wooden tube with a hand-crank attached.

'It's quite easy, really,' said Yorick. He opened a lid on top of the tube. 'You simply pour in the fake snow—just a mix of old goose feathers and some cotton scraps—and I crank the 'andle like my life depended on it. The snow gets blown about very convincin' like, all over Olly.'

Yorick adjusted the angle of the machine before lumbering to the centre of the stage. He picked a lump of chalk from a pocket and drew a cross on the boards.

'Oi, Olly!' Yorick yelled. 'We need to test the snow machine. It took a bit of a knock on the way over from Stratford. Can you take yer mark, there's a good chap?'

Olly Thesp, in the middle of an interview

with Norm Widemouth, was lounging on a chair at the side of the hall. He sighed loudly and rolled his eyes as if Yorick had asked him to work all night digging out a cesspit.

'Oh, very well,' he said, dragging himself across the hall. He stepped onstage and placed an elegant boot on Yorick's chalk mark. 'I suppose we could carry on the interview from here.'

'Very kind of you, I'm sure,' muttered Yorick. 'Waggledagger, grab 'old of the snow, while I gets crankin'.' He indicated a large barrel standing on a prop box. 'On the nod from me, you pour the snow into the machine, right? One barrel should be enough.'

Willy flipped his pigtails over his shoulder and pulled up his sleeves. He was going to be the best fake-snow pourer the Skulls had ever seen.

Yorick began to crank the heavy wooden handle. The snow machine made a powerful whirring sound. When he reached full speed Yorick gave Willy a nod. Willy lifted the lid of the barrel and hoisted it up. It was heavier and smellier than he expected. With a huge effort he up-ended the barrel and poured the contents into the machine.

The machine made a horrid squelching sound and shook violently. Then, with a loud 'plop!', a jet of gunge shot from the machine's mouth and flew across the stage. Willy was sure of one thing: it didn't look like snow. It looked more like a blend of rotten fishguts, cold custard and the leftovers from last night's pickled haggis.

Which is exactly what it was.

The gunge streaked across the stage like a stinky comet. Olly, hearing the gurgling noise, turned to look and took the barrel-load of gunge smack in the face. He somersaulted backwards and landed with a thud.

The gunge missed Norm Widemouth, and

Willy could have sworn the reporter began scribbling notes before Olly even hit the floor.

'What a scoop!' said Norm.

'What a disaster!' said Willy.

'Floop gumble flobber!' said Olly through a mouthful of gunge. He rolled upright, wiping gloop from his eyes and spitting furiously. He staggered to his feet and pointed an accusing finger at Willy.

'You monster!' he screeched. Then he barfed all over Norm's feet and fainted dead away.

Yorick looked at Willy and raised his eyebrows.

'Sorry?' said Willy.

a serPent or two under the flower

The stink from the snow machine emptied the Great Hall of musicians, actors, stagehands and servants in about five seconds flat.

'Wot woz that all about?' said Yorick. 'I 'opes you know we're going to 'ave the devil of a job gettin' this machine workin' again!'

Yorick threw open every window and door while Willy began cleaning up. He placed the barrel upright and began scooping the gunge back into it.

'I don't know,' said Willy, hitching his skirt above his knees and flicking his pigtails out of the way, 'maybe I picked up the gunge barrel by mistake.'

'There ain't no gunge barrel,' said Yorick, his head deep inside the snow machine. ''Old on a minute!' he added, pulling his head out of the machine and squinting at the barrel Willy was holding. 'That's the *right* barrel you got there, Waggledagger.'

He picked a bit of gunge off his beard and pointed to a letter 'S' burnt into the side of the barrel. 'Look! "S" for "snow", see?'

Willy looked at the letter 'S'. Yorick had a point. The trouble was, if this was the right barrel, then someone must have put the gunge into it. Willy peered at the barrel more closely. Near the lid, the wood had been slightly splintered. As if someone had wrenched it off too quickly. Someone using a crowbar.

Willy blinked. There was only one person he'd noticed with a crowbar during the last few hours.

Minty Macvelli.

But there were a thousand reasons for Minty to have had a crowbar. Perhaps he needed to do a spot of emergency repair work on Minimac's mouth. Or maybe he was suddenly overcome with the need to move a large boulder.

'It might have been an accident,' said Willy.

Yorick shook his head. 'That don't make any sense,' he said. 'Why would anyone do summink like that?'

'A joke?' said Willy.

'I didn't see many people laughin',' said Yorick. 'Did you? No, Waggledagger, this woz done for a reason. Someone wanted to create trouble.'

'Trouble for Olly?' said Willy.

'No, fer the Lord of the Fairies, you moon-faced loon! Yes, fer Olly, of course! Who else? Some mongrel nobbled the machine to get at Olly!'

Willy stared at Yorick in horror. 'But that

means someone wants Olly out of action!' he said. 'Why would anyone want to do that?'

Yorick scratched one of his chins and raised an eyebrow. 'I can fink of a few reasons.'

'Maybe he got on the wrong side of a fan,' said Willy. 'Maybe he's got a stalker!'

Yorick shook his head. 'Whoever did this wozn't some loopy fan. This took plannin' and knowledge. This woz an inside job, Waggle-dagger.' Yorick leaned closer to Willy. 'And there's only one person who gains from Olly being knocked out,' he continued. ''S'obvious, really. Minty Macvelli.'

'But he's supposed to be my friend!'

'You got to admit it is quite *likely*. Not that I saw 'im do it, or anyfink.'

Willy didn't want to admit any such thing. 'It can't be Minty!' he said.

'Why not?' said Yorick. ''E will become the lead performer if anyfink 'appens to Olly. 'E *woz* carryin' a crowbar, right?'

Yorick was probably right. But that didn't make Willy feel any better. Willy didn't *want* Minty to be the culprit. He wanted to *like* Minty. He was Minty's lucky charm.

'You must be imaging things, you big galoot!' he said. 'It can't have been Minty!'

Yorick bent down again and began to scoop goop out of the snow machine. 'And jist 'ow, exackly, do you know that, genius?' he said frostily.

Willy didn't answer. He was thinking hard. He did that sometimes.

*

Willy came up with a plan.

As plans went, Willy knew it had more holes than a Swiss cheese, but it was the best one he could come up with: his plan was to keep an eye on Minty.

It seemed like such a simple plan at first. But, after spending some time watching Minty from an uncomfortable perch in the rafters of the hall, Willy was beginning to realise it was, most of all, going to be dull. Minty didn't really do much. If there was a job that needed doing—and in the Black Skulls there was *always* a job that needed doing—Minty would find a way not to be nearby. For the first couple of hours he did absolutely nothing apart from lie around backstage and apply linseed oil to Minimac's head.

Then, just as Willy was beginning to change his mind about the plan, Minty picked up Minimac, checked no one was watching and slipped out of the hall. Willy clambered down from the rafters as fast as he could and headed after him.

Willy followed Minty and Minimac into the main part of Vile Towers, where huge gloomy oil paintings of Sir Victor's ancestors lined the walls. From a quick inspection of their sour-faced mugs it was clear that Sir Victor came from a long line of miseryguts. No surprise there, thought Willy. He hurried past a painting of a particularly po-faced princess petting a Pekinese and turned a corner to find that Minty had suddenly come to a stop and was pretending to inspect the paintings. Willy ducked behind a tapestry.

They were in a grand hallway. At the end was a richly carved door, guarded by two Codpieces. After a few minutes, during which the Codpieces glared at Minty and Minimac, the door opened and a number of official-looking men in black clothes came out. They were talking very seriously. From what Willy could hear as they passed, they had just finished a long meeting about taxes. It sounded very boring.

They had no sooner disappeared from view than Sir Victor emerged. He rushed past Minty without even noticing him.

Willy shrank against the wall as Sir Victor bolted towards him. For a moment Willy thought Sir Victor was going to pull the tapestry aside, but instead he opened a small door nearby and stepped outside. No sooner had the door closed than Minty set off in pursuit, Minimac's head bobbling furiously as he went.

So, Willy thought to himself, Minty has been looking for Sir Victor.

The big question was—why?

Willy stayed hidden and counted to ten. It wouldn't do to follow them too closely. For all he knew, Sir Victor could suddenly decide to turn around and head back. Finally, satisfied that it was safe, Willy opened the door and, after a quick peek, slipped outside.

Willy was half-blinded by the sunlight and it took a few moments for him to see that he was in an empty courtyard. About twenty yards to his right was an arched gate almost hidden by the branches of a chestnut tree. Willy hurried towards it and peeped through.

Beyond it was an enclosed garden of formal flower beds and elaborately trimmed hedges.

Not ten feet away, crouching behind an oversized stone urn, was Minty. He was watching Sir Victor and McDivot enter a small brick building on the far side of the garden.

Willy hardly dared breathe. If Minty turned around, Willy would be a sitting duck.

There was only one option: the chestnut tree.

Willy closed the gate softly, backed into the courtyard and scrambled into the branches of the tree quicker than a monkey with its tail on fire.

He couldn't have chosen a better spot. Willy had a good view of the garden, and he could keep an eye on Minty as well. He sat back against the trunk. He was finding that he was a pretty good spy. All those years of staying one light-footed step ahead of his father's heavy spanking-hand were coming in useful.

For a few moments all was quiet.

Suddenly Minty sprang to his feet. He twitched and trembled, looking right and left. Then, with a squeak of panic, he climbed onto the lip of the urn and dropped down inside, dragging Minimac with him.

Something had spooked Minty. Willy pushed aside a twig, looked across to the other side of the gardens and almost fell out of the tree. Sir Victor was coming back, a garden fork in his hand and a grim expression on his face.

He was heading in their direction.

Fast.

Trotting behind him was McDivot, his ginger whiskers vibrating with tension.

Willy looked around frantically for a better hiding place. Being discovered by Minty was one thing, but Sir Victor was a different game of shove ha'penny altogether. Just as Willy made his mind up to try a suicidal backward somersault into the courtyard, Sir Victor and McDivot came to an abrupt halt.

Sir Victor folded his arms and gazed glumly at one of the fancy flower beds. Almost directly above him, Willy clung trembling to the tree trunk.

'And exactly how long has she been like this?' snapped Sir Victor, pointing at something with the gleaming end of the garden fork.

'Och,' said McDivot, 'that's hard tae say, Yir Lordship.'

Sir Victor leaned over the flowerbed. Willy was so close he could have reached down and plucked the feather from Sir Victor's hat.

'Ermintrude!' murmured Sir Victor as he sank to his knees. 'Oh, Ermintrude, my sweet! What has that ginger imbecile done to you, my precious?'

Ermintrude didn't reply.

Sir Victor wasn't expecting one. Even if Ermintrude had been in the best of health it would have been something of a miracle if she had talked, because Ermintrude was a flower.

Sir Victor scowled up at the quivering McDivot, who looked like he might burst into tears. 'You do understand, McDivot, that Ermintrude is not just *any* flower?' he growled. 'The fact that Ermintrude is the only blue rose ever grown *has* wormed its way into that northern skull of yours, hasn't it?'

McDivot nodded. Up in the tree, Willy shivered. He was glad it wasn't him on the receiving end of Sir Victor's fury.

'Aye, Sir, o' course, Sir!' said McDivot. 'Ah love that flower like she's my own bonny wee thing!'

'I'm just wondering, you see, because it's taken me *eighteen years* to grow a blue rose! And I plan to present that rose to the Queen, which means that Ermintrude must look *perfect*, McDivot, *perfect*! Do I make myself clear?'

'Aye, Sir. Clear as crystal.'

The flower was definitely blue. And it was definitely worth looking at, Sir Victor was right about that. But Willy couldn't see why he was so mad. Ermintrude looked just fine to him. A few slight spots here and there, maybe, but nothing to get steamed up about.

Clearly, Sir Victor had higher standards than most. He took a pair of velvet gloves from his waistcoat pocket, put them on and, as gently as possible, raised the flower's drooping blue head. He inspected Ermintrude closely.

'Absolutely covered in 'em,' he sighed. 'Spots! Blasted spots!'

'Maybe it—Ah mean, *she*—maybe she's got measles?' McDivot suggested hopefully. 'Maybe we could, um . . . wash them or something?'

Sir Victor scowled. '*Wash* them? Ermintrude is a *flower*, you silly little peat-dweller, not a chamber pot! Perhaps we should just *order* the flaming things away! Go on, get out, damned spots! Out, I say! No, you ridiculous, tartan turnip-muncher, there has to be another reason she's not looking her absolute, perfect best. Now, just when I need her to be perfect, she's not. Something's happened and I want to know what it was.'

McDivot frowned in concentration. Then his eyes widened. *'Ooh! Ooh!'* he cried, bouncing excitedly from one foot to the other.

Sir Victor rolled his eyes. 'What is it, McDivot? Spit it out!'

'The actors, Sir!' yelped McDivot, his eyes blazing. 'It's them actors! They've brought a purse on the clace! Ah mean, a curse on the place! Ah can see it all now, Sir! These devilish wizards appear in town and instantly a bleak, black cloud of bad luck and misery falls on us all! Oh woe is us! Cursed are we that——'

Sir Victor smacked McDivot on the back of the head. 'Shut up, McDivot.'

McDivot rubbed his head. 'Aye, Sir. Shut up it is.'

Sir Victor carefully adjusted one of the support canes that kept Ermintrude upright.

'Now go and get some of Ermintrude's special flower medicine from the greenhouses,' Sir Victor ordered. 'Ermintrude must be in tip-top shape to present to Her Majesty tomorrow night. The honour of the Viles is at stake!'

With a last fond glance at the blue rose, Sir Victor marched through the courtyard and back into Vile Towers. McDivot headed in the opposite direction as fast as his little Scottish legs could carry him.

Willy breathed a sigh of relief. He felt like he'd been holding his breath for days.

'What are you waiting for?' said Minimac's grumpy muffled voice from inside the urn. 'They've gone, you big Jessie!'

'I'm trying,' said Minty. 'This urn's bigger than I thought.'

With some difficulty, a very damp Minty clambered awkwardly out of the urn. Thick green scum clung to his hair and bits of leaf mould were stuck to his ears.

'Couldn't you have found a cleaner hiding place, you buffoon?' said Minimac. 'This tunic is ruined!'

Minty didn't reply. He checked the garden for signs of Sir Victor before squelching his way across the path to Ermintrude.

'*That's* Ermintrude?' said Minimac. 'It's a *flower*?'

'You heard him,' said Minty. 'Not just any flower. A very special flower. A flower that means everything to Sir Victor. And he'd be *really angry* if anything happened to it, wouldn't he?'

'Are you thinking what I'm thinking?' asked Minimac.

Minty's eyes gleamed. 'We couldn't,' he murmured. 'Could we?'

'Just do it, you fumble-fingered fool!' snapped Minimac. 'This is your chance!'

Minty dumped Minimac onto the path, took one last glance around the garden, then rummaged inside his tunic. He produced an empty red velvet money bag from one pocket and drew a small dagger from his belt. It glinted nastily in the sunshine.

Willy had a very bad feeling about what was going to happen next. If he was right, Sir Victor was soon going to be even viler than ever.

He groaned softly.

'What was that?' said Minty.

'A bird, birdbrain!' snapped Minimac. 'Now, just get on with it before I pass out from boredom.'

Minty leaned forward and reached out for Ermintrude. There was a crisp *snik* as he cut the stem, and Sir Victor's precious Ermintrude disappeared into the red velvet bag. Then, scooping up Minimac, Minty took off across the lawn like a man who was late for his wedding.

Or his funeral.

As soon as Minty and Minimac were out of sight, Willy clambered down from his hiding place and inspected what was left of Ermintrude. Only a few inches of woody stem remained. He backed away. The last thing he needed was to be found loitering near the scene of a murder. Because that's exactly how Sir Victor would see it. Murder most foul.

As he scurried back across the courtyard there were two things on Willy's mind.

The first brought a blush to his face. What a total idiot he'd been to trust Minty! Yorick was going to laugh his smelly pantaloons off. And now that Minty had gone off his rocker, Yorick was just about the only friend Willy had left.

The second thing was more worrying. What was Willy going to do about what he'd seen? Should he tell Sir Victor? If he did that, Sir Victor would find out that Willy was the boy who'd hidden under the Queen's skirts. His disguise wasn't *that* good and Willy doubted Sir Victor would be forgiving enough to leave Willy unpunished, even if Willy *did* report Ermintrude's murder.

Thirdly, Willy couldn't think of a single reason why Minty would want Ermintrude. Was he a secret flower-collector? A rogue rose-grower?

And lastly, now he had counted up, that was more than two things on his mind. All of them confusing, all of them worrying, and none of them helping.

Life in the Black Skulls was proving to be harder than Willy had imagined.

6

Triple Trouble

The evening light was fading and, as servants hurried along the corridors lighting tallow torches, the rambling chambers of Vile Towers began to flicker with warm orange light.

Inside the door of the Great Hall, Willy caught up with Yorick. Yorick was carrying a coil of rope, the papier-mâché dragon-head and a large sheaf of papers. He looked like a man on a mission.

'Yorick!' cried Willy. 'I—I—I ..., Minty ... the flower ... you were right, he's ...'

''Old up, Waggledagger,' said Yorick. 'I gots a million fings on me plate. Whatever yer blabberin' about now will jist 'ave to wait.'

'But——'

'No buts,' said Yorick. 'Too much to do.' He stomped off towards the stage.

Willy hovered in the doorway, sucking on the end of one of his pigtails.

Now what?

Willy hadn't planned much further than getting back to Yorick and blurting out the whole story. He had hoped Yorick would know what to do, but it looked like he was going to have to wait until after the rehearsal.

But perhaps there was another way to find out what to do next. With a quick glance around the hall to make sure no one was watching, Willy poked his little finger up his left nostril and pulled out a booger. He held it up to the nearest torch and, feeling more than a little silly, closed one eye and squinted at it. But no hidden meanings jumped out. It was just a fairly ordinary booger.

He was squinting with his other eye to see if that helped, when the door leading to the kitchens opened and Minty slipped into the hall. Minimac drooped from one arm and the red velvet bag containing Ermintrude was tucked under the other. Minty sidled along the back wall before heading backstage.

Willy flicked the booger away and set off after Minty. He jumped onto the stage and crossed into the wings. There was no sign of Minty. Willy took a few uncertain steps towards the dressing rooms. There were voices coming from somewhere to Willy's left. He tiptoed closer. The voices were coming from behind the curtains of Olly's dressing room. Willy silently lifted a wooden chair into place beside the curtain, climbed onto the seat and peeked over the top.

Olly was admiring himself in front of a large candlelit mirror. He was quite a sight, Willy had to admit. Shiny scarlet boots, red stockings, vermilion pantaloons, a flame-red leather jerkin, all topped with a big floppy red hat complete with a curving red feather.

'What do you think?' he said to Minty, who was standing behind him. 'Too much?'

Minty shook his head. 'Not at all, Olly,' he said. 'It's *almost* perfect.'

'Almost?' said Olly. 'What do you mean?'

Minimac waggled his wooden head from side to side. 'We-ell,' he said, 'it *is* very red.'

Olly peered into the mirror. 'It's supposed to be red!' he said. 'That's the idea.'

'Oh, we *love* the red,' said Minty. 'Don't we, Minimac?'

The doll nodded.

'It's just that,' Minty went on, 'perhaps it's, well, a little *too* red. Maybe it needs a little something to set it off. A different-coloured something.'

'Something blue,' said Minimac.

Minty dug his hand into the velvet bag and

fished out Ermintrude. He held her against Olly's tunic. 'How about this?' he said, slyly.

Olly flashed his famous, almost-white teeth. 'It's perfect! Where did you find this?'

He snatched Ermintrude and pinned her to his tunic. Then he brushed a braid of hair from his eye and turned back to the mirror. 'You are so right, Minty! That blue is just right! I look *fantastic*. They're going to love me!'

'Yeah,' murmured Minimac. 'You're going to make quite an entrance.'

Willy only just managed to scramble off the chair and hide behind a rack of costumes before Minty and Minimac emerged from Olly's dressing room. Willy sank onto the tail section of the papier-mâché dragon. *This* was why Minty wanted Ermintrude—to put Olly into deep doo-doo with Sir Victor! If Willy knew anything about Sir Victor, it was that he'd act first and ask questions later. Once Sir Victor saw his flower on Olly's tunic, he wouldn't waste time finding out *who* had given Olly the flower. Olly would be lucky to escape this with his head still attached to his shoulders.

It was no use Willy confronting Minty. Minty was taller, bigger and older. And, Willy had to admit, quite scary. Especially when he did that creepy talking with Minimac. Come to think of it, Minimac was pretty scary too.

He would have to think of something else.

Just as Willy's head was beginning to spin with all the thinking, Yorick's voice boomed through the hall. *'Places, everyone! Last rehearsal!'* he bawled. *'Let's make this one a good 'un.'*

Willy decided to put off any more thinking until later. He'd be able to talk to Yorick then and work out what to do. At least this *was* just the rehearsal. Sir Victor wouldn't be watching. There was still time to come up with a plan before Sir Vic's sword hand started twitching.

'Waggledagger!' yelled Yorick. Willy left his hiding place and hurried to the stage.

'Where have you been, you lollygagger?' said Yorick. He pointed to the door. 'Get me my script, sharpish. I left it jist outside.'

Willy pushed open the heavy wooden doors to the vestibule and saw Yorick's well-thumbed script lying on a bench. As he leaned down to grab it, he got the shock of his life. Through a crack in the outer door he had caught a glimpse of the garden beyond.

And spotted Minty.

Talking to Sir Victor.

Willy knew at once that this was A Very Bad Thing Indeed. He inched forward until he was close enough to hear, and pressed an ear against the crack in the door.

'Let me get this right,' Sir Victor was saying. 'You're telling me that the boy I am looking for—that milksop, moon-fed monster; that creature responsible for frightening Her Majesty—is right here in Vile Towers?'

Minty smiled. At least that must have been

what he thought he was doing. To Willy it looked more like the snarl of a wolf. A back-stabbing, double-dealing wolf.

'That's right, Your Lordship. What's more, he'll be taking part in the dress rehearsal.' Minty nodded towards the Great Hall. 'Which is just about to start.'

A vein pulsed dangerously along one side of Sir Victor's forehead.

'Shall we attend?' said Minty.

Willy only just had time to drop to the floor and roll under the bench before the door opened and Sir Victor, his face as welcoming as a wet Wednesday in Wessex, stomped his way towards the rehearsal, closely followed by Minty and a couple of Codpieces.

There was no question about it. Minty was a traitor!

Olly was doomed.

And, thought Willy as he blew a cobweb off his nose, so am I. Double-doomed.

something Very Wicked

It was a disaster. A one-hundred-and-five percent, cast-iron disaster.

Once the coast was clear, Willy rolled out from beneath the bench, darted outside and raced around to the back of the Great Hall. He barged in through the kitchen, past the three hags, who were busy with preparations for supper, and arrived next to Yorick in the wings just in time to see Sir Victor take a seat right in front of the stage. Two Codpieces stood menacingly on either side of him.

'What are you gawking at?' bellowed Sir Victor at Charlie Ginnell. Charlie certainly hadn't expected Sir Victor to drop in for rehearsals and was, for once, stuck for words. 'Get on with it!'

Charlie recovered his poise, bowed as deeply as his belly would allow and signalled to Yorick to start the rehearsal.

Yorick turned to Willy. 'Where've you been?' he growled. 'You almost missed yer mark. Now, get under that stage and wait for the cue.'

Willy opened his mouth to tell Yorick about Minty's betrayal, then remembered that Olly was under the stage, waiting for the catapult to fire him up through the trapdoor. It would be simpler to warn Olly directly.

Willy hoisted his skirt, scuttled down the steps and ducked under the stage, then picked his way between the beams and trestles.

Olly was already crouching on the wooden platform under the trapdoor, Ermintrude standing out against his red clothes like a penguin on an iceberg.

'Erm, excuse me, Mr Thesp,' said Willy.

Olly grimaced. 'You still hanging around?' he said, his voice as cold as a Scotsman's sporran. 'What are you going to do today, set my hair on fire?'

'Ermintrude,' Willy managed to blurt. 'She, I mean, it. They cut her and Sir Victor ... he's going to ... that is, it wasn't me that hit you with the gunge ... I mean, it was, sort of, but somebody ... and I think I know who ... at least I'm sure it's him ... switched the barrels and if you wear the flower, Sir Victor's going to ...'

Olly held up a hand dripping with rings. 'Silence, you prattling fool! What on *earth* are you babbling about? I am, if you hadn't noticed, a *star*. And I need to concentrate if I am going to give of my best! So, shut it, Waggledagger.'

Above their heads, Elbows McNamara's fiddle worked through the introduction. Willy

had only a few seconds before Olly was catapulted onstage with Ermintrude pinned to
his jerkin.

'But, Mr Thesp——' said Willy.

'Not *now*, Waggledagger!' snapped Olly.
'I'm on!'

'But it's about the flower——'

'Never mind the flower! Just do your job,
you blabbering imbecile!'

Willy clung to Olly's sleeve and fixed him
with a desperate stare. 'You don't understand,
Mr Thesp. The flower is *Ermintrude*! Sir Victor's
here! He's going to——'

'Here it comes!' said Olly as the fiddle
reached melting point. 'Pull the lever, idiot!'

Willy couldn't think of anything else to say.

'Now!' said Olly. *'Now!'*

Willy pulled the lever.

There was a blinding flash of white light
and Olly Thesp's boots flew past Willy in a red
blur. The trapdoor snapped shut behind him.

Willy reset the lever and raced up the ladder into the wings. He found a small gap in the curtains and peeped out.

Disaster or not, this he had to see.

As always, even in rehearsals, Olly and the Black Skulls were giving it their best shot. Olly's red outfit gleamed magnificently in the clear strong light that beamed from one of Yorick's powerful candle-and-mirror contraptions. Willy had to admit, the blue rose looked great. The sixty-four-thousand groat question was, what did Sir Victor think?

Willy didn't wait long to find out.

The moment Sir Victor saw the blue rose pinned to Olly's costume, his mouth fell open. He rubbed his eyes in disbelief. A moment later a sound that no one there would forget in a hurry ripped through the Great Hall. 'Noooooooooooooaaaargh!'

It was Sir Victor.

The Skulls stopped playing.

Sir Victor vaulted onto the stage. 'What have you done to her?' he roared, his face reminding Willy of an escaped bear he'd once seen chasing an alderman down Stratford High Street.

Sir Victor snatched the flower from Olly's jerkin with one hand and yanked the actor towards him with the other. He inspected Ermintrude closely, then threw his head back and howled.

'*Eighteen years!*' he yelled. '*Eighteen long years!* And all I have left is this ... this ... *weed!*' He hurled Ermintrude to one side. The flower landed at Willy's feet. Willy glanced down at the blue rose and, right there, the beginning of an idea took root in his brain. He bent down, picked up the flower and slipped it inside his dress. No one noticed. They were too busy watching Sir Victor.

'This will be your last performance, *actor!*' hissed Sir Victor, nose to nose with Olly.

'Tomorrow you've got an appointment with the executioner! That's the usual punishment for *murderers*!'

Olly's face turned sheet-white. 'B-b-but it's just a f-f-flower ... I-I-I- d-d-din't know ... g-g-gave m-m——'

'Silence, drivelling fop!' Sir Victor drew his sword halfway out of its scabbard and, for the eighty-seventh time in his life, Olly fainted.

Sir Victor waved the Codpieces towards the stage. 'Take him away!' he snarled. 'A night in the dungeon and then, once Her Majesty has gone home, he gets the chop!'

'Surely there's been some mistake,' said Charlie Ginnell, stepping forward, his hands fluttering like pudgy birds. 'There's got to be some simple explanation.'

'Don't tempt me, Mr Ginnell,' hissed Sir Victor. 'I have word that this is not the only miscreant in your company! I believe you have a stowaway with you.'

Behind the curtains, Willy shrank further into the shadows, his bottom clenched tightly.

'A boy,' continued Sir Victor. 'A particularly noxious specimen. I will expect him delivered to my dungeons before you leave Vile Towers tomorrow. Now, any questions?'

Charlie shook his head. 'No, Your Lordship. I think that takes care of everything.'

Yorick gave a small cough.

'What is it?' snapped Sir Victor.

'Well, beggin' Yer Lordship's pardon,' said Yorick. 'The Queen ain't goin' to be too pleased that the show is orf.'

'What do you mean, "off"?' said Sir Victor. 'The Queen is *expecting* a show! I refuse to let her down! The show *must* go on.'

'There's the thing, Sir Victor,' said Yorick. 'Olly ain't no ordinary actor. He is the three-times winner of the Strollin' Bones "Best Performer" Golden Lute *and* the fifteen-sixty-eight Elizabethan Idol runner-up!'

'Get to the point,' snapped Sir Victor.

'Wivout Olly there's no show,' said Yorick.

'Actually, Yorick,' said Minty, stepping forward, 'that's not quite true.'

He sloped across to where Olly's red hat lay fallen and picked it up. 'I will take over,' he said. 'After all, I am Olly's stand-in. You won't notice the difference. Except, of course, that I will be better.' He slapped Olly's hat on his head, cocked it at a jaunty angle and flicked the red feather. 'The show will go on!'

'Capital!' said Sir Victor. 'Now get on with it!'

He signalled the Codpieces to pick up the still-unconscious Olly and they stormed out of the door. It slammed behind them with a bone-jarring crash, and Willy felt an icy finger brush against his heart.

The second nose-reading prediction had come true.

8

a Couple of Night Borrowers

It was three bells in the morning. Vile Towers lay silent as the grave, the night as black as a debt collector's heart.

Willy sat on a wooden shelf at the side of the kitchen fireplace and examined his handiwork. Almost there. He stitched a last section of cloth into place, tied off the thread and held the costume up for inspection.

Not bad, thought Willy. Even if it has taken me half the night to make.

He put down the costume and stretched his aching back, bumping his head against the sooty ceiling. It was time to get things moving.

Across the glowing embers on the other side of the fire, the massive lump that was Yorick snored heavily.

Thanks to Yorick's habit of always making himself comfortable, he'd bagged the kitchen digs. Very fine they were, too. Warm, dry, and with vittles aplenty. True, Yorick had to share his bunk with the kitchen goat, and Willy had to sleep on a shelf, but you couldn't have everything in life.

'Wake up,' Willy hissed to Yorick. 'I've got to talk to you!'

'*Maaaa,*' said the goat.

Yorick, who hadn't woken before dawn in nineteen years, groaned deeply and, with a few well-chosen words, told Willy Waggledagger exactly what to do with his suggestion. 'I shall arise,' croaked Yorick, 'when the Good Lord meant me to, which is to say, *not yet*! Besides, I ain't so sure I'm talkin' to you, Waggledagger. Seein' as 'ow you said some 'urtful fings, Waggledagger, most 'urtful. I recall summink about me bein' a big galoot.'

He turned his back on Willy and snuggled up to the goat.

The chances of waking Yorick once he'd closed his eyes were about as likely as persuading a grizzly bear to embroider a quilt. And waking him from his sleep was about as risky as waking that same grizzly, but Willy was made of stern stuff and he didn't give up. He wasn't going to take no for an answer.

Quite simply, he *needed* Yorick.

After slapping Yorick hard across the face for a couple of minutes with no result, Willy finally managed to wake him up by pouring a large goblet of water over his head.

'I *really* 'opes you 'ave a good reason fer doin' that, Waggledagger,' growled Yorick. 'I 'ave been known to 'urt people wot do that kind of fing.'

'Can we leave that until later?' said Willy.

'There's some stuff I need to tell you and some things we need to do. And I'm really sorry I called you a big galoot.'

Yorick sniffed. 'Yeah, well, as I said, that sort of fing can be 'urtful. Specially seein' as 'ow I'm tryin' to trim orf a few pounds.' He patted his gigantic stomach.

'So you'll help?' said Willy.

Yorick groaned and slumped back onto his bed. 'Now?' he said. 'Can't it wait?'

'No, it can't!' said Willy. 'Because Sir Victor is going to *kill* Olly. Until he's dead. With an axe. And, since I know that it wasn't Olly who killed Ermintrude, we have to do something about it.'

'All right,' Yorick said. He knew when he was beaten. 'Let me 'ave it.'

Willy started talking and didn't stop until he'd told the bleary-eyed Yorick everything— the blue flower, the fishguts, the crowbar, Minty's chat with Sir Victor and a recap of Henrietta's predictions.

'Yer sure about all this?' said Yorick, rubbing his eyes.

'Completely,' said Willy. 'And, what's more, I have a plan.' He held up the costume he'd made and brought Ermintrude out from where he'd stowed her on his shelf.

Yorick raised an eyebrow. 'That's the plan?'

'Yes,' said Willy. 'Now get moving, there's a lot to get through. Pretty please?'

*

Almost two hours later Willy was dangling upside down in a leather harness from the ceiling of the Great Hall. He was threading a complicated tangle of ropes through and around the beams that stretched from one side of the hall to the other.

Yorick stood on the floor looking up at him. 'Tighten that one a bit,' he said. 'And put a bit more soot on the one to yer left.'

'Can't we leave it at that?' said Willy. 'All the blood's rushing to my head.'

'No, keep at it, you lazy sprout. The soot's doin' the same fing as when I hid you under the black cloth,' said Yorick. 'If we cover the ropes in soot, they'll be invisible against that black ceilin'. One of the oldest tricks in the book.'

Willy rubbed some more soot along a section of rope. 'Well, I don't know why I have to be the one up here,' he grumbled.

'Two reasons, Waggledagger. First, it's your plan. Second, I'll be blasted if I'm gonna be flappin' about up there with a perfickly good gofer like you lyin' around. Third, it's a bloomin' miracle I'm even agreein' to this load of old tosh.'

'That's three reasons,' said Willy, but Yorick wasn't listening. He was squinting at the ropes.

'Perfick. Can't see a fing,' said Yorick, stifling a yawn. 'Down you come.'

Willy tightened the last of the ropes and wearily lowered himself to the floor. He was almost completely covered in soot. 'Is the costume in position?' he asked. 'And the smudgepots?'

Yorick pulled back a cleverly concealed fold in one of the side curtains to reveal the costume Willy had made earlier dangling from a hidden wire. Close up, it looked like what it was—a few old painted and patched props.

'It'll never work,' groaned Willy. 'It looks terrible!'

'Don't worry,' said Yorick. 'Wiv my lights and mirrors and smoke it'll work a treat.'

'I hope so,' Willy said.

'Not as much as Olly does,' said Yorick, yawning again. 'I'm jist about jiggered, Waggledagger. Olly will 'ave to take his chances wiv wot we've got.'

The first faint fingers of light began to poke through the leaded windows of the Great Hall. If Willy's plan failed, it would be Olivier Thesp's last sunrise.

9

MacVelli Struts Upon the Stage

A large black bear was sitting on Willy's head. He could feel its furry bum pressing him into the floor.

'Help!' yelled Willy, but it was no good. The bear wouldn't get off him.

Then it began to call his name.

'Willy!' shouted the bear. *'Wiiiiillllllyyyyy!'*

Willy tried to open his mouth but it was full of hairy black bear-bum. He was choking.

'Willy!' said the bear again. 'Willy!'

'Willy!' said a different voice.

Willy sat up and blinked. He was under a rack of costumes behind the stage.

Yorick was leaning over him holding a huge fur coat. 'You fell asleep, Waggledagger,' he said. 'Wiv this fing on yer face. And you woz screamin'.'

Willy got to his feet and rubbed his eyes. 'Nightmare,' he said, his voice thick and fuzzy. 'Bear.'

Yorick slung the fur coat back on the costume rack. 'It's a bit of a nightmare situation this side of dream world too. We got a lot to do.'

'I don't know how you two could be so heartless. I mean, sleeping late when Olly's in the clink,' said Charlie. He was crouched a few feet away knitting up the sleeve of the last of his limited-edition Minty Macvelli jerkins. The Black Skulls made almost half of their money from selling this kind of stuff to the fans, and Charlie wasn't going to let a little thing like Olly's imprisonment get in the way of rustling up extra cash. Business was business. He finished the jerkin and put it with the others on the merchandising cart. With some effort he hoisted himself upright. 'This *is* a Royal Performance, too, you know.'

''E was only grabbin' forty winks,' said Yorick.

'Well, be mindful that Sir Victor still expects us to cough up Waggledagger after the show,' grunted Charlie. 'We still have *that* little problem to deal with.'

'We'll fink of summink,' said Yorick.

'Waggledagger! In here ...' yelled a voice from Olly's dressing room.

Yorick snorted. 'We'd best see what 'Is 'Ighness wants,' he said. 'Make sure 'e makes it onstage, eh?' He winked at Willy and headed for Olly's dressing room.

Willy gave one last glance around to check for bears—it had been a very realistic dream—and followed Yorick.

Minty was stretched out on a chaise longue

sucking on a strawberry fool, while the Black Skulls' make-up lady polished his nails. Two slices of cucumber rested on his closed eyelids.

'Don't you fink you should be practisin' the songs, Minty?' said Yorick. 'You know, *rehearsin'*.'

Minty slurped more of the strawberry fool through a straw. 'Of course not, Yorick.' He pointed to his throat. 'An *artiste* must protect his instrument. I don't want to take any chances with my voice. Not today, of all days.'

''Course not,' said Yorick. He glanced at Willy and rolled his eyes.

'Now, I need young Waggledagger for a while, Yorick,' said Minty. 'To run a few errands.'

Yorick scratched his beard. 'Not too much of a problem,' he said. 'I can spare 'im until midmornin'.'

'I may need him for longer,' said Minty.

'Midmornin' it is then,' said Yorick. He

patted Willy on the back, gave him the thumbs-up and clomped out of the dressing room.

'I need a jug of warm chocolate, you lazy young sprout,' said Minty, the moment Yorick had gone. 'Not too hot, mind . . . but not cold either. And get that oaf Yorick to find me a new pair of black velvet pantaloons, there's a good chap. Oh, and would you rustle up a bath?'

'Bath?' said Willy. 'It's not Christmas!'

'Most amusing. Can't appear before the Queen smelling like a ragamuffin now, can I?'

'Oh no, we can't have that!' said Minimac sulkily. He was lying flat on his back in his box.

'And put the lid on Minimac,' added Minty. 'He's becoming very tiresome.'

Willy hesitated. He almost felt sorry for the doll. Minty was betraying Minimac nearly as badly as he'd betrayed Willy. Apart from the fact that Minimac was a doll, thought Willy.

'What are you waiting for?' snapped Minty. 'I'm sick of the sound of him. Besides, he won't be needed any more.'

Willy shut the box, half-expecting to hear Minimac start banging on the lid from the inside.

'Well?' said Minty.

'Well what?' snapped Willy.

'The bath?' Minty clapped his hands twice. 'I'd like it today.'

Willy grabbed hold of a large Chinese vase, lifted it high in the air and brought it crashing down on Minty's head ... At least that's what he would have done if he hadn't had a cunning plan. Instead he nodded and smiled.

'Of course, Mr Macvelli,' he said. 'One bath coming right up.

*

The rest of the day passed in a blur of errands and preparations. Finally, after every rope had been tightened, every footlight and amplifier cone checked and double-checked, and the last of the lines had been memorised, it was almost showtime.

Backstage was buzzing. Along one wall, a long table groaned under the weight of dozens of bottles and various plates of food. Fans were everywhere. Yorick shooed a gaggle of autograph hunters away with a sweep of his gigantic forearm. 'Later, ladies, gents,' he growled at the giggling gaggle of goggling scullery maids and under-gardeners. 'Mr Macvelli and the rest of the lads will be pleased to talk to you *hafter* the performance.'

'Why is *she* allowed in, then?' piped up one of the more persistent fans, a girl with a strong resemblance to a mangel-wurzel.

It took Willy a few moments to realise the girl was talking about him. He was so used to his disguise that he'd forgotten he was wearing it.

'What's so different between her and me? That's what I'd like to know,' said the girl.

'Not a lot,' said Yorick with a sly wink at Willy. 'But, trust me, there is a little difference. Now, scoot!'

With a chorus of groans the maids and under-gardeners scurried back to their duties. Minty, meanwhile, was making more demands.

'I asked for only *black* cherries!' he whined, pointing to a large bowl of fruit. 'They've got horrid little red ones mixed up in there!'

'Aren't cherries supposed to be red?' asked Willy.

'That's the point, you imbecile!' wailed Minty. 'Black ones are harder to get, right? So if I have black ones, it proves that I am more important because people have gone to the trouble of getting them. But, since they haven't, obviously my work here isn't valued! I can't work in these conditions!'

From beyond the curtain Willy could hear the excited chatter from the audience as showtime approached. He peeked through a gap. Every toff within fifty miles of Stratford was there, each in their finest clothes. The Queen sat at a long table in the centre of a packed Hall, Sir Victor at her side. Even from a distance, Willy could see that Sir Victor had plenty on his mind besides the performance. Sir Victor's eyes flicked suspiciously towards the Queen, as if expecting a whole platoon of children to leap out from under her skirts. Here and there massive dogs—lurchers, mastiffs and wolfhounds—snuffled happily through the discarded debris from the pre-performance banquet. The entire place smelled of roasted meat, hot wax, farts and damp dog.

All the ladies carried small bouquets of dried perfumed flowers that they lifted to their noses every few seconds. They needed them.

Especially those ladies unfortunate enough to be sitting near a Codpiece.

The Codpieces were posted around three sides of the hall. Willy gulped. They were on the lookout for him. After Minty's little chat with Sir Victor, they knew Willy was there somewhere. They just hadn't found him yet.

Willy looked up at the ceiling where a thick fug floated above the audience. It was caused by the smoke rising from the candles and torches dotted around the hall. Willy was glad of the smoke. It helped to hide the system of ropes and pulleys he and Yorick had laced through the rafters.

Willy let the curtain fall back into place. He could feel his stomach churning ... and he wasn't even performing.

With a minute to go, the Black Skulls gathered in a tight knot and knocked their fists together. It was a ritual they went through before every performance. Elbows glanced across at Minty, who was admiring himself in a full-length mirror.

'C'mon, Minty, man,' said Elbows. 'Stand-in or not, you're still a Black Skull. Let's do this thing!'

Minty glanced at Elbows's outstretched fist.

'Oh no, I don't think so,' he said after a pause. 'I may mark my lovely glove. Your hands are a little . . . rural for my tastes.'

'All right!' yelled Yorick. 'That's quite enough 'appy banter. We got a show to do.'

He pushed Minty towards the trapdoor while the rest of the Skulls jostled into their positions behind the curtain. Then he gave Willy the thumbs-up and scooted across the stage to shade the footlights. There was a sound like gentle surf breaking over rocks in the Great Hall. It was the sound of a hundred silk-gloved hands clapping and fifty elegant fans flapping. Even toffs got excited when the Black Skulls were in town.

'I say!' yelled the sixth Duke of Birkdale. 'This is ripping, yah!'

'Tally-ho!' squealed the Honourable Lady Amanda Hugenkiss. She whipped out a hunting horn and blew a genteel toot.

'Let one rock!' said the Queen, and punched a fist towards the ceiling.

Showtime!

a DEEd of DrEadful NOTEs

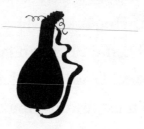

Willy crouched under the stage. Above him Minty Macvelli was thoroughly enjoying himself. Little dust clouds drifted down on Willy's head as Minty pranced across the boards, looking every inch a star as the introduction to the opening song played out.

Make the most of it, thought Willy, crossing his fingers. If my plan works, this could be your last-ever performance.

'Pssst!' hissed a voice.

Willy looked round to see Yorick's shaggy head hanging upside down from the ladder which led backstage.

'All set?' said Yorick.

Before Willy could reply, there was a noise like a cat fighting a porcupine in a bag full of broken china. It was the worst sound Willy had ever heard. It reminded him of the time his father had caught his nose in a mink trap. Yorick's head disappeared from view. Willy scrambled across to the ladder and zipped up the rungs.

'Was that Minty . . . *singing*?' shouted Willy over the din.

Yorick started laughing so hard that one of his few remaining teeth fell out. 'I do believe it woz, Waggledagger! See fer yerself! Minty's jist about the worst singer I've ever 'eard!'

The sound was unbearable.

Elbows, his fiddle arm still busy, glared at Minty. But Minty had his eyes shut and didn't notice. Charlie Ginnell was in the wings making frantic 'keep playing' motions with his arms. Walden Kemp had his hands clamped over his ears and his mouth open in a perfect 'o'. The drummer, Perce Coop, picked up a spare drumstick and pinged it towards Minty's head. It missed.

The Queen, owner of the stiffest upper lip in all of England, showed exactly why she was Queen. Only her make-up cracking here and there revealed that she was hearing anything other than a sweet, tuneful melody. Sir Victor—a man who had fought at the Battle of Nobbin-on-the-Naze and single-handedly captured an enemy town armed with only a stick and a rolled-up laundry list—also showed he was made of sterner stuff than most. He simply inserted the ends of his magnificent moustache into his ears.

Everyone else went nuts.

Lady Loudtrouser, Sir Victor's elder sister, began stuffing small oranges in her ears while Lord Loudtrouser dropped to the floor and tried to pull his own head off. A large Codpiece began crying like a baby. Viscount Cedric Cholmondley-Biscuit-Ffyffe crammed his head up the backside of a roast swan. The Countess of Manchestershire, a large lady, fell to the floor in a dead faint, crushing her lady-in-waiting.

It was pandemonium.

Meanwhile, Minty sang on, eyes closed, blissfully unaware that he was stinking up the joint.

'He can't sing!' yelled Willy.

Yorick took his fingers out of his ears. 'This goes *way* beyond "can't sing", old chum. This is worse than Rat Miggins in last years' Roadiebury Fest talent contest. And Rat Miggins doesn't even 'ave a tongue!'

Suddenly a tomato arced across the footlights and smacked into Minty's shoulder.

The audience had clearly had enough.

When a mouldy potato knocked Minty's hat off and a three-week-old cabbage bounced

off his forehead, even he began to suspect that things were not going exactly to plan.

Minty soldiered on until a dagger landed, point first, two inches from his right boot. He finally got the hint: the audience didn't like him. He stopped singing. The band stopped playing.

The silence in the Great Hall was broken only by the sobs of the wounded and a low moan from Viscount Cedric Cholmondley-Biscuit-Ffyffe.

From the side of the stage Charlie Ginnell drew a finger across his throat. 'Enough!' he hissed.

Yorick grabbed a rope and, for the first time ever, lowered the curtain early on a Black Skulls performance.

Bravely, Charlie Ginnell stepped in front of the curtain to face the audience.

'What is the meaning of this, Mr Ginnell?' The Queen's voice cut through the moans of the audience, many of whom were gingerly getting back to their feet. 'Is this some sort of *joke*?'

'Of course, Your Majesty,' Charlie said, trying to bow but not managing because of his belly. 'Unfortunately, it doesn't seem to be very funny. So, with your kindness, there will now be a short intermission after which we will go straight into tonight's play, *The Sheeted Dead*!'

The Queen narrowed her eyes. 'Very well, just so long as there is no more appalling noise!'

'Of course not, Your Majesty!' said Charlie. He smiled glassily, bowed again and waddled back between the curtains.

'*What was that?*' Charlie hissed at Minty, who was removing rotten vegetables from his hair.

'You useless twonk, Minty!' said Yorick.

'I can't help it if you peasants don't recognise *genius* when you hear it!' said Minty.

'That's it!' yelled Charlie. 'I'm going to

strangle him!' He lunged at Minty, grabbed him by his collar and pushed him up against the wall.

'Stand aside!' cried Walden Kemp, darting from the prompt box and beating Minty over the head with a rolled-up script.

Yorick picked Walden up by the scruff of his neck so that Walden's little legs kicked furiously in midair, then put a massive hand on Charlie's chest and pushed him aside.

'Steady, chaps,' he said quietly. 'If you get rid of Mr Wonderful 'ere, who'll go onstage? You?'

'Yorick's right!' gabbled Willy. He could see his carefully worked-out plan disappearing before his eyes. If Charlie dragged Minty off-stage now, all his effort would have been for nothing. 'Minty has to go on! He must! There's no singing in the play! It'll be fine!'

Charlie snorted. 'This is your last chance, Macvelli,' he hissed. 'If there was anyone else—*anyone*—able to play the part, you'd be out of here faster than you could say "sacked"! This time there will be *no* nasty surprises. Do I make myself clear?'

Minty nodded.

'On in five,' yelled Yorick.

Willy wiped his brow. That had been close. Now all he had to do was put the plan into action.

all Hail MacVElli

Minty was slumped in a chair in his dressing room. 'They *hate* me,' he muttered to Willy, whose job it was to get Minty ready to go back onstage. 'I mean they *really* hate me! They threw a *dagger*!'

He looked towards Minimac's box. 'Why didn't *you* ever say anything about me not being able to sing?'

'I'm a *dummy*, dummy!' said Minimac. 'And in case you've forgotten, you abandoned me. You won't get any help from me!'

Minty moaned. 'This is it,' he said. 'I can't go on.'

'You have to,' said Willy. 'There's no one else!'

'I don't care!' Minty wailed. 'I quit!'

Willy rubbed his face and readjusted his wig. Minty *couldn't* quit. Not *now*. Not if the plan to save Olly was going to work. Then he had an idea. Not a great idea, admittedly, but it would have to do.

'Wait here,' he said to Minty, and darted in the direction of the kitchen.

Hermione, Hortense and Henrietta were making fried-badger sandwiches.

'How's it all going?' said Henrietta as she expertly stripped the meat from a large badger. 'It sounds very exciting!'

'No time to explain,' cried Willy. 'You have to come with me. We need you!'

Henrietta held up a badger leg. 'Now?' she said. 'We're far too busy, young man. It'll have to wait.'

Willy stamped his foot in frustration. Then

he flung himself on the floor and grabbed Henrietta by the ankle.

'Please!' he wailed. 'You have to help me! I'm desperate! Desperate, I tell you! Triple pretty please with extra honey?'

Henrietta looked down at him. She wiped her hands on her apron. 'Well,' she said, 'since you put it like that, I think we could at least take a look, eh, girls?'

Willy jumped to his feet. 'Quick,' he yelped. 'Put your better foot forward! Swift as an arrow, and all that. There's not a moment to lose!'

'That boy needs to work on his dialogue,' murmured Hortense. She gestured to her sisters. 'After you.'

'No, after you,' they said.

'Oh, hurry up!' said Willy. 'Don't worry about who goes first! Just go! At once!'

Hermione gave Willy a frosty look. 'We're going, young man. In our own time, wisely and slow. They stumble that run fast, you know.'

Eventually Willy got the hags out of the kitchen and into Minty's dressing room.

'This is all I need,' groaned Minty as the hags pushed through the curtain. He pointed at Henrietta. 'This is your fault. Everyone hates me. I wish you'd never told me I was going to become the lead performer!'

'Our fault?' said Henrietta. 'Isn't this what you wanted?'

'Well, yes,' said Minty. 'I suppose I did.'

'The thing is,' said Willy, keen to steer the conversation back towards getting Minty out on the stage again, 'Mr Macvelli has somehow got the silly idea that he's not going to carry on. I just wondered if there was anything you could tell him to change his mind?' He smiled at Henrietta and crossed his fingers behind his back.

Henrietta didn't answer. Instead she wiped some badger goop off her fingers and, before

Minty could protest, expertly thrust a wizened finger up his nose and pulled out a booger. She held it up to the dressing-room candle and looked at it closely.

'Hey!' cried Minty, holding his nose.

'What does it say?' said Willy, hardly daring to breathe. His neck might depend on what Henrietta saw in Minty's booger.

'Some interesting stuff,' Henrietta said to Minty. 'It says that no man can stop you. There's something else here, too. You will remain lead actor with the Black Skulls until flowers talk.'

Minty sat upright. This was more like it.

Willy squinted at the booger on the end of Henrietta's finger. 'It says all that?' he asked.

Henrietta flicked the booger over the dressing room curtain. It landed unnoticed in the bowl of cherries.

'The boogers don't lie,' she said. 'Now, if you'll excuse us, we've got to finish those badger sandwiches or we'll be late for broomstick practice.'

'Only kidding,' said Hortense, with a wink.

'Broomstick practice is *Thursday* nights,' said Hermione.

The hags chortled and scuttled out.

'You hear that, Mr Macvelli?' said Willy as the curtain closed behind them. 'Your booger is telling you to get back onstage and show everyone what you—the multi-talented minstrel Minty Macvelli—are made of! No man can stop you!'

Minty stood up. 'You know what, Waggle-dagger?' he said, his eyes gleaming. 'I do believe you're right!'

He flung aside the curtain to his dressing room and strutted out to where Yorick, Charlie, Walden and the rest of the Skulls huddled anxiously. They looked up as Minty pranced towards them.

'Watch out, world,' said Minty, putting his

hands on his hips and jutting out his chin. 'Here comes Minty Macvelli!'

'Glad to hear it,' said Charlie, mopping his brow with a silk handkerchief. 'Now get back in that dressing room and put your costume on!'

'But remember,' growled Walden, his face as red as a beetroot, 'one wrong move and you'll wish——'

'Keep your powder dry,' Minty said with a wolfish grin. 'No man can stop me now!'

Willy wanted to punch the air. Instead, he smiled sweetly at the man who'd betrayed him to Sir Victor, the man who'd murdered Ermintrude, the man who'd put Olly Thesp in mortal danger.

This was revenge, and it was going to be fun.

Shake Those Gory Leaves

As it turned out, once Minty Macvelli got back onstage, he wasn't half bad.

''Is actin's pretty good,' whispered Yorick, who was on stand-by with a large sheet of stiff parchment that was used to make the noise of thunder. 'Fer a low-down, skulkin' scoundrel.'

'It couldn't have been much worse than his singing,' said Willy. 'And he's right where we need him to be: onstage.'

Willy peered through a gap in the curtains to see how the audience was responding. One or two lords and ladies still had bread rolls jammed in their ears, but most rolls were being removed as Minty began to move skilfully through his lines. Even Sir Victor took his moustache out of his ears and sat back in his seat. He couldn't be described as relaxed but he didn't look like he was about to chop anyone's head off, either.

'Everything set?' whispered Yorick.

'Don't forget we'll need to put some of those candles out,' said Willy, indicating the lights at the back of the audience.

Yorick nodded his shaggy head in agreement. 'Let's get moving.' He put down the parchment and slipped around the side of the hall to put out the candles and torches. Soon the room was in almost complete darkness.

Minty stood in a single shaft of green light beaming up from a hole in the stage. Yorick lit a smudgepot, and Willy picked up a set of bellows, aimed them at the pot and began to crank. Ghostly smoke drifted across the stage.

'Oh, hideous ghoulie!' whispered Minty 'Spare me! Oh, spare me!'

Queen Elizabeth, Sir Victor, the assorted toffs and the Codpieces watched open-mouthed. Lord Loudtrouser, whose attempts to remove his own head had, thankfully, failed, clutched Lady Loudtrouser's arm and chewed his nails. McDivot, who'd sneaked in at the back for a quick peek, had his fingers laced in front of his eyes. Even the lurchers and mastiffs were hooked.

You could have heard a very small pin drop.

In the shadows behind one of the side curtains, Willy had dropped the bellows and was doing his best to squeeze Yorick into the costume he'd made the previous night.

'It's too tight!' hissed Yorick as he tried to heave himself inside. He huffed and puffed, bending this way and that. Willy fetched a fishslice from the buffet table and used it like a shoehorn to slide Yorick in. Then, in desperation, he crammed the top half of the costume over Yorick's head and hung from it with all his weight.

'Ow!' said Yorick. 'Yer bendin' me lugholes!'

Willy gave up. It was like trying to put a pint in a half-pint pot. 'I told you not to eat that goat!' he whispered. 'Very fattening, are goats.'

'I woz *'ungry,'* said Yorick. 'Besides, that goat snored, you know.'

'Be quiet!' hissed Willy. 'They'll hear you.'

'It's no good,' said Yorick. 'You'll 'ave to do it!'

Yorick removed his left leg from the costume—the only bit he'd managed to put on—and handed it to Willy.

'Me?' said Willy.

'We're runnin' out of time,' said Yorick. 'And I'm better at 'andlin' the ropes, anyways.'

'What if——' Willy began.

But before he could finish, Yorick had whipped off Willy's wig, picked him up, stuffed him into the lower part of the costume and rammed the top half over Willy's head.

Then, with a few deft movements, Yorick attached the costume to the harness and hoisted Willy into the air. 'Perfick fit,' he said.

'Oi!' said Willy trying his best not to panic as he rose upwards. 'It's dark in here!'

'Use the eyeholes,' said Yorick. 'An' keep quiet, fer cryin' out loud!'

Willy wriggled his head until he found the eyeholes. It *wasn't* a perfect fit, but it was better than being unable to see. Yorick kept hauling on the ropes and Willy rose in a series of jerks towards the ceiling. Pretty soon he was higher than the gantry Yorick had rigged up for the stage curtain.

The audience will see me too early, he thought, in a sudden panic.

He needn't have worried.

Every eye in the place was locked on Minty as the big moment approached.

'I beseech you, foul beastie of the underworld,' Minty wailed, waving his arms. 'Appear now, or forever be banished!'

Willy glanced down as Yorick lit another smudgepot and thick green smoke began to billow across the stage.

'Oh, I say!' said the Queen, pointing upwards. 'One is most thrilled!'

A shape was beginning to materialise out of the smoke.

It was Willy.

He began to drift towards the stage, the luminous paint Yorick had used to touch up the costume glowing eerily. Lady Amanda Hugenkiss cried out. Lord Loudtrouser fainted.

Minty rubbed his eyes. He knew a ghost was supposed to appear at this point in the play. But it should have been nothing more than a sheet draped over a stick, controlled by Yorick standing in the wings.

This ghost wasn't a sheet. There was no stick.

Instead, Minty watched transfixed as a ghastly, ghostly, green-glowing, obviously dead-as-a-doornail gigantic blue rose—its leaves ragged and singed, its once-lovely blue petals hanging limply—floated effortlessly in his direction.

It was Ermintrude.

Or, to be more accurate, Ermintrude's ghost.

Peering through the eyeholes, Willy saw that Minty was terrified. Willy positioned his mouth against the amplifier cone sewn into the costume and got ready for his lines. He unfurled a tattered leaf and pointed it at Minty's quivering face.

'Ah, my old friend, *Macvelli*,' moaned Willy. 'I've been meaning to have a word with you.'

The amplifier cone, lightly stuffed with muslin, made his voice sound like someone speaking with a mouth full of mashed turnips.

But to Minty, there was no doubt: this was Ermintrude back from the grave to haunt him. His teeth chattered. His knees knocked. His eyes boggled. If his ears could have flapped, they would have.

'Wh-wh-what d-d-do you w-want?' he finally squeaked.

'The truth, Macvelli, just the truth.'

'I—I—I, th-th-the t-t-t-t-t-t-tru-tru . . .'

Willy drew a deep breath and let rip with everything he had. *'Murderer!'* His muffled voice echoed around the Great Hall. *'MURDERER!'*

If someone had inserted a live firework in Minty's undergarments, the effect could not have been more dramatic. He squealed like a four year-old and fell heavily to his knees.

'I'm sorry! I'm *sorry*!' he moaned miserably.

'For what?' said Willy, anxious that no one should miss the point. 'What are you sorry for you miserable, um, minstrel?'

'It was me!' wailed Minty. 'Me and Minimac! He made me do it! It was all his idea! *Please don't hurt me!*'

'Made you do what?' asked Willy.

'Kill you!' cried Minty.

'Ouch!' said Willy as the harness gripped his tender bits a little too tightly. 'I mean, *aaargh*, *grrrr*, I'm really angry!'

Minty didn't appear to have noticed any-thing strange. He grovelled on the floor. 'I did it all! I cut you down! I persuaded Olivier Thesp to wear you onstage! It was me! All *meeeeeee!*'

From the Queen's table there was a noise like steam escaping from a geyser.

It was Sir Victor. 'Unspeakable varlet!' he roared, leaping to his feet and pointing his sword at Minty. 'Monstrous wretch!'

'Quiet!' hissed the Queen. 'One is enjoying this, Vile! Put back your sword and sit down. This instant!'

For a second Sir Victor looked like he might risk an appointment with the executioner's axe by arguing with the Queen. Then, with a superhuman effort, he replaced his sword in its scabbard and sank back into his seat, his eyes glinting dangerously.

One of the Codpieces made his way through the crowded tables to Sir Victor. 'Beggin' yer pardon, me Lord,' he muttered out of the side of his mouth, 'but if *this* bloke 'ere is the one wot cut yer flower, then what do you want us to do wiv the *other* bloke? The one in the dungeon?'

Sir Victor hadn't thought of that. The Queen would not be happy if he cut off her favourite actor's head. Especially if the favourite actor turned out to be innocent.

'You haven't cut off his head yet, have you?'

'No, Yer Lordship,' said the Codpiece.

'Then bring him here at once.'

The Codpiece saluted and headed for the dungeon.

'One is warning you, Vile!' hissed the Queen. 'Another interruption and you are for the Tower!'

Sir Victor smiled apologetically. It wasn't something he was very good at. He looked more like a man trying to pick a piece of meat from between his teeth with his tongue. 'Apologies, Your Majesty, it won't happen again.'

The Queen turned her attention back to the stage, where Minty now cowered in a trembling heap.

Meanwhile, Willy was getting more and more uncomfortable. Then, as he shifted around inside the costume for the hundredth time, there was a loud ripping sound. The ropes holding him up snapped and he dropped like a stone, right on top of Minty.

The audience screamed.

The Queen clapped excitedly. 'Oh, most amusing!' she laughed.

'*Aaaargh!*' screamed Minty. He scrabbled frantically to get out from under Ermintrude, convinced that the zombie flower was trying to kill him. With a last desperate push he heaved himself clear, dislodging the top half of Willy's costume as he did so.

Willy sucked nice clean air into his lungs and wiped the sweat from his face.

Minty Macvelli goggled. 'You!' he squeaked hoarsely. 'You're not a ghost! You're my . . . my lucky charm.'

'You're right, I'm not a ghost, Minty,' gasped Willy. 'But you may want to rethink that "lucky charm" part.'

Minty glanced towards the backstage area, scrambled to his feet and took off like a scalded cat.

13

The Hurlyburly's almost Done

Sir Victor, seeing Ermintrude's killer about to make his escape, was unable to sit still for a moment longer, Queen or no Queen. He exploded across the table like a ball from a musket and caroomed towards the stage, his eyes fixed on Minty's retreating back. Roaring the ancient battle cry of the Viles, he barged Lord Loudtrouser out of the way and, using Viscount Cedric Cholmondley-Biscuit-Ffyffe's head as a trampoline, sprang onto the stage. He caught up just as Minty was exiting stage left and slammed into Minty's knees, sending him crashing sideways into a stage flat.

'My knee!' wailed Minty, clutching his leg.

Sir Victor leapt to his feet. 'Prepare to die most horribly, you pestilential, plant-plucking peasant!' he snarled, whipping out his sword.

Minty cringed and wrapped his hands around his head.

Sir Victor shot a glance at Willy. 'And don't think I've forgotten about you, me laddo!' he added. 'I'll deal with you once I've cleaved this miserable miscreant in twain!'

'Please!' cried Minty. 'I don't want to be twained!'

Sir Victor curled his lip and brought down his sword in a vicious arc, straight at Minty's thin white neck.

'Enough!' The Queen's voice cut through the hall like a wire through ripe cheese. 'That's quite enough, Vile!'

Sir Victor froze, the edge of his sword a hair's-breadth from Minty's neck.

The Queen got to her feet and clapped.

Everyone else immediately did the same.

'Bravo! What a performance!' the Queen said. 'The best entertainment one can ever remember seeing! One is very impressed!'

Sir Victor gaped at her. 'Have you gone completely m——' he began, then stopped, remembering in the nick of time that the Queen *was*, after all, the Queen. He quickly rearranged his face into what he hoped was a pleasant smile, but in fact made him look like a man who had found a ferret in his pantaloons.

With one last volcanic glance at Minty, Sir Victor lifted his sword from Minty's neck. Minty collapsed on the boards.

'You are such a *clever* little Lord,' said the Queen. 'Thinking all this up by yourself.'

Sir Victor pointed his sword at Willy. 'Are you sure I can't chop this one's head off, Madam? This *is* the boy we found hiding under your petticoats, Madam,' he said with gritted teeth.

'*Too* funny, Vile,' said the Queen. 'There's no need to carry on the performance any longer. I have to say, you certainly know how to put on a good show! I haven't laughed so much since Raleigh lost his pantaloons at Plymouth! I mean, talking ghost-flowers! How amusing!'

'Ah, well, yes, quite,' said Sir Victor, putting his sword back in its scabbard. 'One tries to please, don't you know?'

'Did it take long to set up?' asked the Queen. 'How did you manage it, exactly?'

Sir Victor looked desperate. 'Um, er . . .'

''Is Lordship spared no heffort in makin' Yer Majesty's visit a pleasurable one,' said Yorick, stepping forward from the wings. 'He got us to rig up some hexplosions, create an oversized flower costume to 'is personal design, and then use a series of stage wires and pulleys to recreate the "floatin'" heffect. Ain't that right, Sir Victor?'

168

Sir Victor coughed. 'Um, yes, exactly. Just like the hairy peasant said.'

Willy winkled Ermintrude from inside his tunic, turned and shuffled to the front of the stage—it was quite difficult to walk in the flower costume—and held the rose up to the light. 'As a token of his affection for Your Majesty,' Willy said, 'Sir Victor Vile would like to present you with this special souvenir of the entertainment: the only blue rose in the world! A blue rose for the Red Rose Tudor Queen.'

Willy passed Ermintrude to a Codpiece who handed it to the Queen.

'A magnificent gift, Vile!' said the Queen. 'You are *such* a clever little Codpiece!'

Sir Victor bowed so low his forehead almost scraped the stage. 'You are too kind, Your Majesty.'

'Far too kind, if you arsks me,' muttered Yorick in Willy's ear. 'Ruddy bloke didn't do anyfink.'

Before Willy could reply there was a buzz of activity at the back of the hall. The doors flew open to reveal a wild-eyed Olly with a Codpiece at each elbow. Looking a lot like someone who had spent the last couple of days hanging upside down in a smelly, rat-infested dungeon, he tottered through the crowd towards the stage, his hand nervously fingering his neck. He guzzled gratefully from a goblet of wine that Baroness Milksnatcher gave him, and then signed autographs for the Earl of Wingnut's children.

Norm Widemouth appeared out of the throng, parchment and quill in hand. 'Any word for our listeners, Olly?' he said. 'Was the preparation for this role difficult?'

'What role?' said Olly.

But Olly was never to find out because the crowd pushed him forward to the Queen's table. He blinked at her for a moment before bowing unsteadily.

'Ah, Mr Thesp,' said the Queen. 'Now that you've joined us—very good prisoner-costume you have there by the way, Mr Thesp, most convincing—I would like to invite you to Richmond Palace for my summer entertainment. One is quite taken with you Black Skulls chappies. Would that be convenient, Mr Thesp?'

Olly didn't answer at once. He was still dazed, and was also looking over his shoulder, trying to make sense of the scene onstage where Minty was writhing on the floor, holding his knee; Sir Victor was standing around looking confused; and Willy was dressed, for some reason, as a giant flower.

'So I'm not going to have my head chopped off?' he said, turning back to face the Queen.

The Queen simpered. 'Very good, Mr Thesp! Of course not! Now, my offer?'

Dazed as he was, even Olly knew there was only one answer to an offer from the Queen. 'We'd be honoured, Your Majesty.'

Sir Victor still hadn't given up on Minty. 'What about this one, Your Majesty?' he said, waving a hand at Minty who had staggered to his feet. 'I'd really, really like to chop his head off. You wouldn't miss him.'

'You are silly, Vile,' said the Queen. 'There's no need to keep up the performance now. Of course this chap must come to the palace. His part in all this has been quite delightful.'

'As you wish, Madam,' growled Sir Victor.

'Until Richmond, then,' said the Queen. She gave a royal wave, turned and sailed regally towards the doors, followed by her retinue.

'Toodle-loo, Vile,' she called over her shoulder. The doors closed behind her and she was gone.

The rest of the toffs immediately began grabbing their hats, gloves, earmuffs and fans and headed for the doors themselves.

Willy turned and started shuffling back-stage, taking a route that avoided Sir Victor, who was still standing, twitching, at the centre of the stage. Willy had almost made it to safety when a familiar voice cut through the air.

'WILLLLLLL-*IIIIIAAAM*!'

Willy stopped dead in his tracks. There was only one voice like that in the world. His father's.

He turned to see his father standing at the back of the hall. Beside him was his mother wearing a long black gown.

She wiggled her fingers at Willy. 'Hello, sweetie!' she said. 'It took us absolutely ages to find you! We had to pretend to be Lord and Lady Shakespeare! It's all been very exciting, darling!'

'Never mind that namby-pamby "darling" nonsense, woman!' yelled Willy's dad. The vein on the side of his head was throbbing like a snake trying to swallow a pig. Willy knew that meant his father's hands would be itching with pent-up bottom-spanking energy.

'What's the blethering idiot doing dressed up as a *flower*? I *knew* it would come to this! Get rid of that *unmanly* costume right now, William Shakespeare! And what do you mean by associating yourself with these common *actors*?'

Willy opened his mouth to explain but nothing came out. He was, as always, tongue-tied when his father was shouting.

Yorick came to the rescue. 'The lad means no 'arm, Mr Waggledag——I mean, Mr Shakespeare. 'E 'as been a great 'elp to us all.'

The vein on Mr Shakespeare's forehead pulsed dangerously.

'What a load of old tripe. If my wife wasn't so soft-hearted I'd have you all locked up for kidnapping! We *work* for a living round here. None of this fancy, prancing, acting, theatre nonsense for the Shakespeares! We've been tanning hides for generations! Hundreds of years from now, when folk say the name

"Shakespeare" it'll be fine gloves and honest boots they'll be thinking of, not the theatre! The theatre's nothing more than a pack of thieves and liars! Mark my words, it won't last!'

That was fighting talk where Yorick was from. He laced his fingers together, flexed his arms and cracked his knuckles. Then he jumped heavily from the stage and strode meaningfully towards Mr Shakespeare.

Charlie Ginnell, moving surprisingly fast for such a large man, grabbed Yorick by the elbow.

'Leave it, Yorick,' he said quietly. 'The lad belongs with his parents.'

Yorick snorted but didn't move any further. Charlie was right.

'Sorry, kid,' Charlie said to Willy. 'Nothing we can do about it.'

Willy eased himself off the end of the stage and shuffled miserably in the direction of his parents, Ermintrude's leaves dragging sadly along the floor.

'So long, Waggledagger,' said Yorick. 'It's been a blast.'

Mr Shakespeare grabbed Willy roughly by a leaf. 'Wait till I get you home, young man!' he growled, heading for the door.

'Bye!' said Willy's mother. 'Lovely to have met you all!'

The doors closed behind them.

It was all over.

14

whEN shall WE TWO MEEt again?

The Black Skulls packed up before dawn the next day, and were on the road faster than an oiled eel on ice. It was a long haul to Richmond and they didn't want to waste time. The line of heavily laden carts creaked down the track and away from Vile Towers.

Behind them shuffled a solitary figure. It was Minty. He scooped up the tenth bucket of ox poop for the morning and slopped it in a sack with the rest. Charlie Ginnell, always on the lookout for a way to earn a fast groat or two, planned to sell the bags of poop to dedicated fans as Genuine Black Skulls

Fertiliser. It was a stinky, embarrassing job, and it would be Minty's all the way to London.

'Having fun back there?' shouted Olly over his shoulder. He chuckled and lay back against a sack of wigs. His memories of the ordeal in the dungeons seemed to be fading fast as Vile Towers dropped away in the distance.

Yorick sat at the reins of the lead cart. Behind him, most of the crew were perched wearily on bundles of curtains, boxes of props, and the thousand-and-one items the Black Skulls needed to keep the show on the road.

The goat from the kitchens sat next to Yorick on the riding board. Yorick, of course, had not eaten it. He never ate goat for breakfast.

On the other side of Yorick, Charlie Ginnell was counting the takings.

'No cash from Vile,' he said, 'but we sold plenty of souvenirs, and at least we got the Richmond Palace gig!'

'True,' said Yorick. 'And it woz all young

Waggledagger's doin'. It woz 'im wot put the plan together. 'Im wot fixed up all the wires and smoke and wotnot. 'E's a natural whizzbang when it comes to theatre. I'm gonna miss the whelp.'

Yorick brushed away a fly that had flown in his eye. At least, that was what he would have claimed if you had asked him.

'Yes,' said Charlie, 'it's a shame his dad turned out to be such a——'

'Bustard!' yelled Yorick. He pointed at a large bird that flew across the road and spooked the oxen. 'I 'ate those bustards.'

The wagons creaked into Stratford and out the other side. The last house in High Street was Willy's. Yorick could tell from the smell. Tanner's houses always reeked.

Mr Shakespeare stood scowling at the front door. Behind him, Mrs Shakespeare, her hand stuck up a chicken's bum, waved cheerily. 'Toodle-loo, Mr Yorick!' she trilled.

Yorick waved back at her, and scowled back at Mr Shakespeare.

'You don't frighten me!' yelled Willy's father.

'Yokels,' muttered Yorick.

'Maa!' said the goat.

'Don't you start,' said Yorick.

As he turned away for the last time, he glanced at an upstairs window and saw Willy. Yorick waved, but Willy took no notice. He was staring sadly into space.

'Poor kid,' Yorick muttered.

He cracked the reins and the oxen lurched forward. Then he reached inside his tunic, fished out his emergency slice of eagle pie and wolfed it down in one mouthful. He always turned to food in times of stress. Leaving young Waggledagger behind was proving to be one of those times.

'Eagle pie, eh?' said Charlie. 'Not like you to get attached, Yorick. An old stager like yourself.'

Yorick picked an eagle feather from between

his teeth. 'There woz summink about that lad,' he muttered. 'It took summink special to come up wiv that whole Ermintrude ghost fing. Summink *theatrical*. An' now 'e's gonna spend the rest of 'is life tannin' hides and gettin' 'is hide tanned. Wot a waste.'

There was a loud bottom-sound from one of the oxen and Minty scurried round to scoop up the poop that followed.

'You missed a bit there, Minty,' said Yorick.

Minty scowled and bent to scoop up another dollop.

'Never mind, Minty,' piped a voice from the back of the cart. 'Only six more days to go.'

'Aye,' said Olly. 'And then you and that doll——'

'Hey, wait a minute!' said Yorick. 'I know that voice.' He turned to see Willy peeking out from under a bundle of black cloth.

'Waggledagger!' cried Yorick. 'Wot are *you* doin' 'ere? I fort I saw you . . .'

Yorick glanced back at Willy's house where Willy's head still drooped sadly in the upstairs window. 'I don't understand,' he said. ''Ow ...?'

'Misdirection,' said Willy. 'A wig on a wig-stand, a few props. Oldest trick in the book.'

Yorick reached back a hairy arm, grabbed Willy by the scruff of his jerkin and dragged him onto the riding board. 'Give the lad room, Charlie!' he said.

Charlie scrambled into the back of the cart, punching Willy playfully on the arm as he passed. 'You are full of surprises, Waggle-dagger!' he said.

'Welcome back, you crafty little whipper-snapper!' bellowed Yorick, before sticking a grimy finger up his nose and pulling out a booger the size of a small bird. He looked at it and made a face. 'Remember those predictions the 'ags made?'

Willy ducked as Yorick flicked his booger into the road. 'About Minty becoming the stand-in and all that? How could I forget?'

Yorick nodded. 'Well, don't forget they also predicted plain ole Yorick 'ere would discover the greatest theatrical talent of all time!'

'And did you?' Willy asked, making himself more comfortable between Yorick and the goat.

'Well, you never know, Waggledagger,' laughed Yorick. 'Maybe them 'ags woz right.'

'You never know,' said Willy.

'Stranger fings 'ave 'appened,' said Yorick.

He cracked the reins and the oxen lurched into top speed. They creaked past an old man carrying a haystack on his back.

'No sleep till Little Hetherington on the Wold!' shouted Yorick, punching the air.

'Rock and roll!' yelled Willy.

'What?' asked Yorick.

'The cart,' said Willy. 'It's rocking and rolling.'

'Get used to it,' said Yorick. 'Yer in the theatre now, Waggledagger.'

about the author

Martin Chatterton has traced his family tree back to the days of William Shakespeare and, in an amazing coincidence, has found that the greatest English playwright was not his great-great-great-great-great-great uncle! Born in Liverpool, only a stone's throw from Stratford (assuming the stone was launched via a grenade launcher), Martin has been doing joined-up funny writing for absolutely yonks. Martin loves Shakespeare because if the Bard was ever stuck for a word the cheeky monkey would just invent one! Martin's favourite Shakespearean word is 'road'.

about the artist

Gregory Rogers was born in Brisbane, Australia, which is nowhere near Stratford. His favourite Shakespeare play is *A Midsummer Night's Dream* because it's got such great characters. Like Shakespeare, Gregory loves inventing good characters and in over 20 years of illustrating books he's created lots. One of his books even won the prestigeous Kate Greenaway Medal in England. He bets Shakespeare never got one of those!